Off Off Broadway
Festival Plays

Thirty-Sixth Series

BEDFELLOWS
by Adam Peltzman

THE TRUTH ABOUT CHRISTMAS
by Daniel Pearle

HANKSYLVANIA
by Travis Helwig

MOUNTAIN SONG
by Josh Beerman

PLUCK AND TENACITY
by Daniella Shoshan

MY NAME IS YIN
by Tom Swift

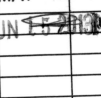
A Samuel French Acting Edition

SAMUEL FRENCH

FOUNDED 1830

NEW YORK HOLLYWOOD LONDON TORONTO

SAMUELFRENCH.COM

ISBN 978-0-573-70020-0   Printed in U.S.A.   #20251

MUSIC USE NOTE

IMPORTANT BILLING AND CREDIT
REQUIREMENTS

36th Annual
Samuel French
Off Off Broadway
Short Play Festival

The Lion Theatre • Theatre Row • NYC
July 19th-24th

FOREWORD

We are very honored to present these six daring and inspirational playwrights as the winners of our 2011 Off Off Broadway Short Play Festival. This year, we broke Festival records with over 1,000 submissions from across the country. From that initial submission pool, we've indentified these six gifted playwrights who use humor, insightful characters, and riveting stories to confront important social and human issues. We thank them for sharing their talents with us and welcome each one into the Samuel French, Inc. family.

The vital relationship between playwright and theatre is one that we know well at Samuel French. Whether producing a Tony-winning play or developing a new work, theatre companies play a vital role in cultivating new audiences and communicating a playwright's vision. We commend them for this mission and thank each of the forty producing companies involved in the 2011 Festival for their tireless contribution and dedication to their playwright.

Perhaps the most challenging part of the OOB Festival is our production week. From our initial pool of Final Forty playwrights, we ultimately select six plays for publication and representation by Samuel French. Of course, we can't make our selection alone, and so we enlist some brilliant minds within the theatre industry to help us in this process. Each night of the Festival, we have an esteemed group of judges consisting of a Samuel French playwright, a theatrical agent, and an artistic director. We thank them for their support, insight, and commitment to the art of playwriting.

Samuel French is a 181 year-old company rich in history, while at the same time dedicated to the future. Much like the innovative playwrights involved in our Festival, we are constantly striving to develop groundbreaking methods which will better connect playwright and producer.

On behalf of our board of directors, the entire Samuel French team in our New York, Los Angeles, and London offices, the over 10,000 playwrights, composers and lyricists that we publish and represent...we present you with the six winners of the 2011 Samuel French Off Off Broadway Short Play Festival. Get ready to be inspired.

The Festival Organizers
Samuel French 36th Annual Off Off Broadway Short Play Festival
Samuel French, Inc.

The Samuel French Off Off Broadway Short Play Festival started in 1975 and is one of the nation's most established and highly regarded short play festivals. During the course of the Festival's first 35 years, over 500 theatre companies and schools participated in the Festival, including companies from coast to coast as well as abroad from Canada, Singapore, and the United Kingdom. Over the years, 204 submitted plays have been published, with many of the participants becoming established, award-winning playwrights.

Festival Coordinator: Kenneth Dingledine
Production Coordinator: Billie Davis
Literary Coordinators: Katy DiSavino & Roxane Heinze-Bradshaw
Web/Print Content Coordinator: Amy Rose Marsh
Press/Public Relations: Ron Lasko, Spin Cycle
Graphic Design: Gene Sweeney
Lighting Design: Miriam Crowe
Technical Advisor: Eric L. Beauzay
Stage Manager: Casey McLain
Festival Staff: Joe Ferreira, Sara Mirowski, Teresa Ronquillo, Molly Bagby, Richard Patterson, Jonathan Donahue, Laura Lindson, Alicia Grey, Jake Glickman, Matthew Akers, Tammy Sellner, Josephine Messina, Joe Garner, Alice Roth, Abby Colella, Jamie Lamchick, and Alex Rankine

SAMUEL FRENCH STAFF

Managing Director: Nate Collins
Director of Finance: Rita Maté
Director of Marketing and Acquisitions: Abbie Van Nostrand
Director of Licensing Development: Brad Lohrenz
Director of Licensing Operations: Lori Thimsen
Contracts Manager: Lysna Marzani

GUEST JUDGES

Susan Bernfield	Kia Corthron	Jonathan Lomma
Beth Blickers	Cusi Cram	Jonathan Mills
Adam Bock	Paige Evans	Thomas Pearson
Bekah Brunstetter	Mark S. Hoebee	Lloyd Suh
Matthew Burnett	Barbara Hogenson	Alexis Williams
Kevin Cochran	Katherine Kovner	Jeff Zinn

CONTENTS

BEDFELLOWS

A Comedy
(based on a true event)

by Adam Peltzman

Bedfellows was produced as part of the 36th Annual Samuel French Off Off Broadway Short Play Festival at the Lion Theater at Theater Row in New York City on July 19, 2011 and July 24, 2011 as part of the Festival Finals. It was directed by Sarah Jenkins, with costumes by Erin Dougherty. The cast was as follows:

JOHN ADAMS. . . . . Gary Marachek
BENJAMIN FRANKLIN. . . . . Zenon Zeleniuch

CHARACTERS

JOHN ADAMS – a bit uptight
BENJAMIN FRANKLIN – a free spirit

TIME

Autumn, 1776

PLACE

An inn in New Brunswick, New Jersey

AUTHOR'S NOTE

Bedfellows is based on a night in 1776 when John Adams and Benjamin Franklin were forced to share a bed in a crowded inn. The two men were en route to New York to meet with the British general William Howe when they stopped for the night in New Brunswick, New Jersey. The inn was practically full and a room with a single bed was all that was available. After getting into bed Adams and Franklin squabbled about whether the room's window should be opened or closed (Adams had a cold and wanted to close it; Franklin craved fresh air and wanted it open). The disagreement prompted them to have a spirited debate about the cause of the common cold.

This incident forms the basis of the play, and a couple of phrases, pulled from historical accounts, are worked into the dialogue. But the play is by no means meant as an accurate historical reenactment, as many liberties are taken with the facts for the sake of comedy (as just one example, there's no evidence of Franklin wearing a gown to bed, but it's a funny image so I wrote it into the play). Accounts of the actual event can be found in numerous books, including David McCullough's excellent biography, *John Adams.*

ABOUT THE AUTHOR

Adam Peltzman is a New York-based writer for the screen and stage. He is an Emmy-winning children's television writer and has served as head writer on a number of series, including *The Electric Company* and *The Backyardigans*. Adam is also the creator of several television pilots currently in production. Adam's short comedic play, *Jest for the Day*, was a finalist at the 2011 New York City 15-Minute Play Festival at The American Globe Theatre. Other produced stage work includes an adaptation of *The Backyardigans*, which toured nationally in 2008. Adam has years of experience doing improvisational comedy and is a graduate of Wesleyan University. He lives in Brooklyn, NY with his wife, Sarah.

(The stage is dark. Revolutionary War era fife and drum music underscores the following narration.)

ADAMS. *(narration)* My dearest Abigail. I hope this letter finds you in good health. I am battling a stubborn cold myself. We're halfway through our journey to New York to meet with the British command and have stopped for the night at an inn in New Brunswick. The inn is fully occupied, leaving Dr. Franklin and myself to share quarters that are gravely, gravely insufficient.

(Lights up on a small room, with only a small bed and a nightstand. ADAMS – fully dressed in colonial attire – finishes his letter on the bed, looking miserable. FRANKLIN – wearing a nightgown, hums a patriotic tune as he wipes his teeth with a rag. He shimmies a bit. ADAMS looks up at FRANKLIN, then goes back to finishing his letter.)

ADAMS. *(writing)* God grant me the strength to endure this ordeal. Your beloved, John.

(ADAMS puts away his writing materials. FRANKLIN continues to wipe his teeth throughout the following.)

FRANKLIN. I've always loved New Jersey! You, Adams?

ADAMS. It's fine.

FRANKLIN. I just find it agreeable. Wouldn't you agree that it's agreeable?

ADAMS. It's not disagreeable I suppose.

FRANKLIN. I'm particularly fond of the folks along the coast.

ADAMS. Yes, it is a high class of people on the Jersey shore.

FRANKLIN. *(offers rag to ADAMS)* Salt rub?

ADAMS. I'll pass.

FRANKLIN. Suit thyself, but clean, strong teeth are the mark of a clean, strong man. Ooh, that has a nice ring to it. I smell a new book coming on. *Dentistry and the Soul of Man.* I think I'll write it Tuesday.

(As FRANKLIN *bends to put away his rag, his gown creeps up.)*

ADAMS. *(wincing)* It's nearly winter, Dr. Franklin, how could you wear that dress?

FRANKLIN. It's a gown, Adams. Please don't emasculate me. Plus, I don't care what season it is – I need to let Poor Richard roam free, if you know what I mean.

ADAMS. Well, I find this room rather chilly. I'll remove my wig and that's it.

(He removes his wig.)

FRANKLIN. Hmm. I don't find it cold. Sure, the room could benefit from a Franklin Stove…

ADAMS. *(mutters to himself)* Oh dear God.

FRANKLIN. What?

ADAMS. I deplore when you do that.

FRANKLIN. Do what?

ADAMS. Call it a Franklin stove.

FRANKLIN. Well that's what it's called. I invented it.

ADAMS. Yes, I know you invented it – I've been hearing that story since the 1750's. But you're Franklin. You could just call it a stove.

FRANKLIN. Fine. This room could benefit from a stove. Happy? Dear me, Adams, what's gotten your knickers in a bunch?

ADAMS. What do you think? Look around! How many beds do you count?

FRANKLIN. *(looks…counts)* One…one I suppose. So? You've never shared a bed with your fellow man?

ADAMS. No offense, Doctor, but we're not exactly the slimmest of revolutionaries.

FRANKLIN. *(pulls down on robe)* Hmmph. Speak for yourself. What, would you prefer that waif Jefferson for a bed-fellow?

ADAMS. I think not. His flatulence is well-documented.

FRANKLIN. Well, we seem to be at an impasse, Adams.

ADAMS. Nonsense. There is a floor. I have a coin.

(pulls out a coin from his pocket)

Call it in the air, Doctor – pine tree or Indian.

(flips coin)

FRANKLIN. *(reluctant)* Indian.

ADAMS. *(catches)* Pine tree. Sweet dreams.

(**ADAMS** *gets into the bed, on his side, facing away from* **FRANKLIN.***)*

FRANKLIN. You scoundrel, I won't have it.

(**FRANKLIN** *squeezes into the bed.* **ADAMS** *sits bolt upright.)*

ADAMS. What are you doing?

FRANKLIN. Taking my rightful place in this bed.

ADAMS. You lost the toss!

FRANKLIN. I never consented to the tossing of coinage to begin with. Dear sir, might I remind you that I'm nearly 30 years your senior? How will it appear to Congress when they hear that you forced Big Daddy Franklin to the floor?

ADAMS. Big Daddy? Who calls you Big Daddy?

FRANKLIN. I just made it up. I can't stop inventing things.

ADAMS. Fine. Fine. You may remain. But some provisions, Doctor. We are to face in opposite directions. Neither is to cross this central meridian. And snoring must be kept to a minimum.

FRANKLIN. So many rules. Shall we draft a treaty?

ADAMS. No need to be flip. Good night.

FRANKLIN. See you on the morrow. Oh. Let me just take off my bifocals. Which I invented. Ah, that was a good day.

(He removes his bifocals and reaches over **ADAMS** *to put them on the nightstand, then takes a moment to settle into bed.)*

FRANKLIN. *(softly to himself)* Early to bed, early to rise, makes a man healthy, wealthy, and wise.

ADAMS. Are you quoting yourself?

FRANKLIN. Just a little something I like to say before bed.

(They both settle in to go to sleep. After a moment, **FRANKLIN** *sits up slightly, sniffs at the air with displeasure, and then looks up at the sole window in the room. He gets out of bed and opens the window.* **ADAMS** *bolts upright again.)*

ADAMS. Have you lost your mind?

FRANKLIN. No, I'm relieving the stale air in this chamber.

(takes deep, cleansing breath)

The night air is invigorating! I could write a poem. Or invent a major social institution.

ADAMS. Okay, Doctor. The chamber is relieved, close the window.

*(**FRANKLIN** returns to the bed.)*

FRANKLIN. I think not. The window shall remain open.

ADAMS. It shall not.

FRANKLIN. Shall.

*(**ADAMS** climbs over **FRANKLIN**, gets out of bed, and goes over to the window.)*

ADAMS. Shalln't!

(He slams the window shut.)

FRANKLIN. Adams! To close the window at night will destroy a man's procreative powers.

ADAMS. I'll have you know that I've fathered five children.

FRANKLIN. That, sir, only proves that the age of miracles has not passed.

(He stands to go back to the window but **ADAMS** *blocks his path.)*

ADAMS. Dr. Franklin – with all due respect. I already have a slight cold and don't wish it to get worse.

FRANKLIN. *(a realization)* Oh. Ohhhhhhhhh….

ADAMS. What?

FRANKLIN. It all makes sense now. Have you not read my theory of colds?

ADAMS. Oh, that. Yes, I think I borrowed it from the lending library once.

FRANKLIN. The "Franklin" lending library, please.

ADAMS. Well I thought it was nonsense. And I do not need a "theory" of colds. I have an actual cold. If you'd like to read my "theory" take a look in my handkerchief.

FRANKLIN. Mmm. And do you sleep with the window open or shut?

ADAMS. Shut, of course.

FRANKLIN. Thank you for proving my theory. Zing, my dear friend. Zing indeed. Now move aside.

ADAMS. *(holds firm)* No! It stays closed.

FRANKLIN. *(thinks, then points)* Ah, Betsy Ross! What are you doing here?!

ADAMS. What?

(As he turns to look **FRANKLIN** *bolts around him and opens the window.)*

ADAMS. You son of a scallywag.

FRANKLIN. Come, come to bed. I shall convince you of my theory of colds. If I cannot, you may close the window. Deal?

*(***ADAMS*** *sighs and mutters. They go to the bed and settle in.)*

So, tell me – what do you think causes colds?

ADAMS. You know…damp vapors. In the cold air.

FRANKLIN. Damp vapors? That is adorable. I must pinch your cheeks.

ADAMS. Please don't.

FRANKLIN. *(does)* Too late. How old fashioned of you! Do you also write your letters with a chisel and tablet?

ADAMS. No. You know I use a quill, I'm up on the modern advances.

FRANKLIN. Well, let me enlighten you further. Cold air does not produce a cold in man. I've tested it myself. I've been out in the freezing air many a time, and quite scantily clad, and have not caught cold.

ADAMS. *(mutters)* I'm sure Poor Richard loved that one.

FRANKLIN. People catch colds from each other, Adams. From being shut up in coaches, or small rooms, and from sitting near and conversing so as to breathe in each other's transpiration.

ADAMS. Oh, wonderful. So let's sit near and converse in a tiny bed. I must have your transpiration all over me.

(frantically wipes himself)

FRANKLIN. *(springs out of bed – an oration)* Ah – but that's where the fresh air comes in. Fresh air is the antidote, Adams! Fresh air disperses the transpiration. Fresh air is the sole defense against the contagion. Don't you see the beauty in that? The very thing we thought caused the ailment, in fact guards us against it. And how do we know? Inquiry. Investigation. The enemies of superstition and baseless fear. That, John John, is why I love the age of reason. Isn't it incredible? Provide me with five.

(He holds up his hand out to be slapped.)

ADAMS. *(glares, dumbfounded)* Provide you with five?

FRANKLIN. Yes, just a little gesture I invented to celebrate something. We can try an elevated five.

(He raises his hand for a high-five. **ADAMS,** *at wits end, gets under the covers and has a tantrum.)*

ADAMS. Aaaaaaah!!!

FRANKLIN. What? You don't believe the theory?

ADAMS. *(pops out)* To the contrary. It makes perfect sense. Every word. It's brilliant.

FRANKLIN. Oh. Well you have a funny way of showing it.

ADAMS. You know what the problem is with you, Dr. Franklin?

FRANKLIN. I have a problem?

ADAMS. For all your achievements…for all your worldly experiences…there is one thing you will never achieve. There is one experience you will never, ever be able to know.

FRANKLIN. And what's that?

ADAMS. Sharing a bed with Benjamin Franklin! I've never felt so appreciative of my wife. She is a learned woman. She knows a thing or two. But when we lie in bed at night, I can say, "Abigail, I took a ride to the lending library today" without her saying, "Oh, that's interesting, because I invented that ground-breaking institution!" She didn't invent the bifocals…or the hospital…

FRANKLIN. *(blushes)* That was a good one.

ADAMS. …or the odometer. Or the glass harmonica. Or the fire department…

FRANKLIN. *(wistful)* Seemed so obvious at the time.

ADAMS. Yes, well, why didn't I think of it? Good night, Dr. Franklin. Keep the window open.

(**ADAMS** *settles into bed.* **FRANKLIN**, *in bed, taps him.*)

ADAMS. *(turns)* What?

FRANKLIN. You forgot the lightning rod. Kind of a biggie.

(**ADAMS** *sighs and turns away.* **FRANKLIN** *lies there, looking a bit hurt.*)

FRANKLIN. If it's really that annoying…I guess I could stop achieving things.

ADAMS. No. Don't be silly. Truth be told, Doctor, I quite admire your work. You're a great American, and a true patriot. Just a pain in the posterior to sleep with.

FRANKLIN. Aw. Thanks, John-John. That's sweet.

(pause)

You know, you're a mighty fine patriot yourself. *Thoughts on Government* was a real page turner.

ADAMS. *(turns around)* Really?

FRANKLIN. Oh yes. A couple of dangling participles here and there, but it's inspired work. Truly.

ADAMS. *(warmly)* Oh. Thank you, Doctor. That means a lot.

FRANKLIN. Good night, Adams.

ADAMS. Good night, Dr. Franklin.

*(They both settle in and close their eyes. The lights begin to fade. **ADAMS** falls quickly asleep, as **FRANKLIN** lies awake.)*

FRANKLIN. Ooh. It is a bit brisk.

*(**ADAMS** starts to snore.)*

The only cure for that is human warmth.

*(**FRANKLIN** turns and spoons **ADAMS**.)*

Hmm. That's interesting. Our forms are nestled like two utensils in a drawer. We're utensiling. No, too general. Forking? Sounds dirty. Spooning. Yes, that's what I shall name it. Good one, Big Daddy. Good one indeed.

*(**FRANKLIN** snuggles up to **ADAMS** and closes his eyes. A soft version of a patriotic song – such as "The Star Spangled Banner" – plays like a lullaby, as the lights fade.)*

The End

THE TRUTH ABOUT CHRISTMAS

by Daniel Pearle

The Truth About Christmas was produced as part of the 36th Annual Samuel French Off Off Broadway Short Play Festival at the Lion Theater at Theater Row in New York City on July 22, 2011 and July 24, 2011 as part of the Festival Finals. It was directed by JV Mercanti. The cast was as follows:

SHELLY MCALLISTER . . . . Julie Boyd

LORI BERGMAN . . . . Sarah Koestner

BERTA LEVINSON . . . . Kelly McAndrew

JANINE PALMER . . . . .Katya Campbell

REMY MCALLISTER . . . . Jessica Ranville

CHARACTERS

SHELLY MCALLISTER, 40s, Remy's mother
LORI BERGMAN, 40s, Lindsey's mother
BERTA LEVINSON, 40s, Courtney's mother
JANINE PALMER, 30s, guidance counselor at The Patterson School for
    Girls
REMY MCALLISTER, 14

TIME

A few days before Christmas.

NOTE ON DIALOGUE

A slash (/) denotes point of interruption by the following speaker.

NOTE ON PERFORMANCE

With the exception of Remy, all characters address the audience. The
four women exist in separate worlds. When Remy speaks, she addresses
other characters as indicated, moving among them like a ghost.

ABOUT THE AUTHOR

Daniel Pearle grew up in Los Angeles, California. He earned his BA from Harvard College and is finishing his third year as an MFA candidate at The New School for Drama. Plays include: *Plunder* (winner of the 2008 Loeb Drama Center's Phyllis Anderson Prize); *Moon Watch* (St. Fortune Productions); *Alone Upon the Earth: A Love Song*, *Three Women Against the Sea*, and *Freefall*. His play, *Bel Canto*, was given a reading at Primary Stages as part of their Primetime Reading Series and is currently a semifinalist for the 2012 Eugene O'Neill Theater's National Playwrights Conference. Residencies/Conferences include: Blue Mountain Center, New York State Summer Writers Retreat, UCLA Writers Studio.

(**REMY** *sits at a desk, her back to us, hunched over a book. She clicks on a lamp. A laptop and other open books and papers are spread out in front of her.* **SHELLY, LORI, BERTA,** *and* **JANINE** *address the audience.*)

SHELLY. Two weeks before the Patterson fire, I saw Lori Bergman coming out the front gate at school. She was wearing this black wool topcoat, everything all done up, you know, very Lori. And I wasn't going to say anything, I had nothing to say to her, but just as I'm about to cross her path she stops me and says: "So. Shelly. I hear your daughter's waging a war on Christmas." Like it was a joke. Like it was funny.

LORI. I didn't mean it as a *joke.* I mean we used to be close, Shelly and I. When she first enrolled Remy at Patterson, we'd meet for lunch every other Tuesday, this little sushi place up on 86th. And she'd go on and on about the problems they'd had with other schools – socially, academically – because Remy was so special, so unique. Shelly thought a girls' school would be better for a kid like that – smart, very smart, but struggling to make friends. She'd done her research, she'd read the articles. At the time I thought she was sweet, a little insecure maybe but I never would have imagined –

BERTA. My husband wants to sue. They think they can *expel* my daughter after eight years, because some antisocial narcissist with overly permissive parents starts telling lies?

SHELLY. And don't start me on Berta Levinson. She always hated Remy, even back when our girls were friends.

BERTA. I think what I resent is – My daughter Courtney was severely dyslexic – IS severely dyslexic. And it was hard. It was really hard. I mean this may sound crazy to you but I remember first grade Lori Bergman threw a birthday party for Lindsey and when it came time to unwrap presents they made each girl read her card out loud. And Courtney couldn't do it. She wasn't reading yet. And the looks on these mothers' faces... It was like she had *the plague* or something. And were any of those mothers sympathetic? No. Of course not. I mean there were girls who wouldn't invite her over for play dates if you can believe it. But Courtney didn't let that drag her down. She didn't take out her frustration on everybody else, even as a kid. Which, if you ask me, is exactly what Remy was doing.

(**REMY** *hurls some pages off her desk. Under the following dialogue she slowly, methodically begins to pin up her hair.*)

JANINE. Look, Patterson is a highly competitive school. Someone is always cutting herself, someone is *always* suicidal, let's not even get started on the senior girls applying to college, who are all over-medicated by that point.

SHELLY. Those girls, those mothers. They'll tell you Remy set that fire. Like it's been proven, like it's a fact. And they certainly *won't* tell you what went on before.

JANINE. I mean it's not like I'm new at this, I worked as a guidance counselor downtown for six years before coming to Patterson, but it's just such a different world, these parents – the money they spend, the *pressure* they –

LORI. Sure, it was difficult when the girls had their fallout, but frankly Lindsey was very mature about the whole thing – she said, "Mommy, Remy McAllister is just not growing into the kind of person I want to associate with." Thirteen years old.

JANINE. And let me tell you these girls *lie*. Okay? They lie right to your face.

LORI. Most girls that age would talk behind her back, but Lindsey was honest and brave enough –

SHELLY. Remy came home crying, all flushed and red-eyed, slammed her door, I heard her breaking things –

BERTA. Who even remembers what it was? It was middle school! Kids recover. They're not made of *glass*.

JANINE. I remember I heard Courtney Levinson once in the girls' bathroom with a finger down her throat – I mean trust me I know what that sounds like – and so I called her into my office and sat her down, this fourteen-year-old girl with her manicured nails and her collarbones peeking through her skin and she says, "Oh no, Dr. Palmer, don't worry, I've been a little stressed 'cause my parents might be getting a divorce but I'm taking good care of myself I *swear*." And I'm sitting there with my little Buddhist rock garden on my desk and my Zen water fountain bubbling in the corner and I'm thinking: You manipulative little bitch.

(beat)

LORI. I heard they fired Janine Palmer. The guidance counselor. And maybe that's too bad but she's an adult. Lindsey is fifteen, what am I supposed to tell her?

BERTA. Courtney's had her heart set on Stanford since her internship in Palo Alto two summers ago. Do you know what this looks like? On her transcript?

SHELLY. "You're just not the kind of person we want to associate with," that's what Lindsey told her. No reason, no explanation, nothing. And I don't care what they tell you, *that's* when this started, because I bet it got Remy thinking – about scapegoating and group psychology. She spent the whole summer at the library or on her laptop, meanwhile she wouldn't talk to us. And I can understand the girls at school might have been confused when she came back, they might have been curious, but she wasn't breaking any school policy, she wasn't doing anything wrong, I mean for God's sake it was just a *headscarf*.

REMY. *(turns around)* It's not a headscarf. It's a Hijab.

*(We can see now **REMY** is wearing a Muslim Hijab.)*

JANINE. She corrected me. That was the first thing she said in our meeting. I mean it was all very confusing.

BERTA. What was confusing? The girl was desperate for attention…

JANINE. Because I knew she'd been getting funny looks –

REMY. That's not what this is about.

SHELLY. She was expressing herself. What was I supposed to tell her?

LORI. I mean you can't blame the girls – the sight of it was ridiculous…

SHELLY. She said she was a Muslim.

BERTA. She's probably a *lesbian.*

LORI. Her purple backpack slung over one arm, her designer jeans, walking around the Upper East side with this *thing* on her head…

BERTA. Not that I care, I'm just saying –

JANINE. And she'd written this – manifesto. It was five pages single-spaced.

SHELLY. Listen to me, I did not *encourage* her. It's obviously not something you expect, watching your child go through a – Muslim phase – and of course I didn't want her getting hurt but on the other hand I was glad to see her *passionate* about something again, something she cared about –

JANINE. And I'm reading it right there in my office and I say, Hold on, Remy, I'm confused – Is this about the Hijab or about the Christmas tree?

REMY. *(to* JANINE*)* This is about *Patterson* – "An independent secular institution, not associated with any creed or religion," that's directly from the mission statement.

BERTA. And Shelly was almost *boastful.* Like clearly this was evidence her daughter was so remarkable, like who else but Remy would pick up the *Koran* for summer reading?

SHELLY. You have to understand, Patterson had a *reputation.* They valued independent thinking – that was their whole *thing.*

BERTA. …if only *our* girls could be as precocious and open-minded –

REMY. This is *not about me*. This is about the administration's decision to endorse something completely at odds with everything Patterson claims to value.

LORI. *(scoffs)* Please. The girl starts wearing a *headscarf* to school, and no one, not the school, not the other kids, no one tells her maybe it's not the place, no one mentions Jamie Lazarcheck whose father *died* in the World Trade Center, not *one person* gets in her way and suddenly she turns around and starts attacking the school for having a *Christmas tree?*

REMY. It's *hypocrisy!*

LORI. It's *insane*.

BERTA. There's something to be said for not treating your daughter like Queen Elizabeth from the time she's potty trained.

JANINE. She'd posted this thing on all the school message boards. She'd scheduled meetings with the Dean.

SHELLY. And they *loved* Remy when she interviewed. They saw her potential. She'd had four schools in five years and finally, *finally*, at Patterson she seemed happy. She was applying herself. She was making friends. We thought: *Thank God*. A school that *gets* her. A school that *understands*. / A school that –

REMY. *(reads)* "A school that claims to educate girls to think for themselves, to go against the grain, to speak critically about our world, to *not* just follow the crowd...

JANINE. She must have spent hours –

REMY. ...And what could be more antithetical to this philosophy than the tacit endorsement of uniform commercialized 'holiday cheer' that a Christmas tree – *any* Christmas tree – represents?"

BERTA. It's fucking *festive* for crying out loud!

LORI. It's a school-wide tradition. All the Elementary school girls, grades K through 6, they make these adorable decorations, construction paper and glitter, then the seventh graders take them and hang them up –

BERTA. And there were dreidels too! There was no sign that said, "Happy Birthday Jesus."

SHELLY. I tried to tell her, I said, "Honey, it's not religious, it's decorative."

REMY. *(to* **SHELLY***)* It's a *symbol.* Of consumerism, of waste, of all the things we should be *ashamed of* as Americans...

LORI. The war on Christmas.

BERTA. The Christmas Jihad.

SHELLY. Well I'm sorry I *did* tell her I was proud. Okay? She was making a case for something she believed in, something she knew would be unpopular...and I told her. I said, "Sweetheart I'm proud of you."

LORI. I saw it on Facebook. Lindsey got me on Facebook last summer, it was *her* idea, I'm not one of those mothers who browses her kids' photos all horrified and titillated, you know, it was just for fun, and anyway I could see it in the whaddyacallit, news feed: "Remy McAllister joined the group..." – what was it – "White kids for Islam..."

BERTA. Remy McAllister: "likes the Koran."

SHELLY. But the abuse she suffered.

JANINE. Look, I was not ignoring the problem –

SHELLY. I saw the note. Someone shoved it in Remy's locker. In big sharpie, on a piece of graph paper, someone had written the word: "Terrorist."

LORI. Lindsey was *worried* –

SHELLY. *Terrorist.* What kind of bigoted Upper East Side brat thinks it's funny to call someone –

BERTA. Courtney told me, she said, "Remy's made new friends. Outside school. She's full of rage."

SHELLY. My daughter came home *bleeding.* All right? From her *scalp.*

JANINE. We'd had several meetings. Even before –

REMY. It was pinned, Dr. Palmer. It was carefully pinned.

(**REMY** *holds the Hijab in her hands. There's blood on it.)*

SHELLY. Lindsey Bergman and Courtney Levinson, they came up behind her in the cafeteria –

LORI. No one saw it happen –

BERTA. Courtney is not some bullying *thug*!

JANINE. It was very difficult to know just how much of / this was –

BERTA. She has spent two summers interning at the NYU fertility / clinic. How –

LORI. Lindsey is smart, compassionate, open-mined –

REMY. *(to* **JANINE***)* Do you see this? Do you?

SHELLY. They ripped the thing right off her head!

REMY. I'm *bleeding.*

BERTA. Listen to me, Samantha Haggarty *saw* Remy in the girls' bathroom pulling out her hair –

SHELLY. They were kicking her, she was on the ground –

BERTA. It was *self-inflicted.*

JANINE. The school has a very strict zero tolerance policy / when it comes to anything resembling bullying –

LORI. I mean how does this happen? Everything Lindsey's worked / for –

BERTA. Do you know what tuition costs? Eight *years* of tuition?

JANINE. Expulsion was not my decision. But I had an / obligation tell the administration –

SHELLY. My *daughter was attacked!*

LORI. I *did not raise a monster!*

(Beat. **REMY** *turns upstage. Under the following dialogue,* **REMY** *begins slowly and quietly packing up her bag.)*

JANINE. That was two weeks before the Christmas tree was set on fire.

I was in my office – I smelled smoke and heard screaming – and by the time I got there the alarm had gone off, Mr. Sexton was holding the fire extinguisher, there was this white foam everywhere, and the entire bottom half of the tree was just – naked. All charred and black and ashy.

SHELLY. No one even saw Remy. There was no evidence. In this country we don't presume guilt, do we? And what about the other girls? Lindsey? Courtney? They had motive, didn't they?

LORI. I was horrified, what do you want me to say?

BERTA. At some point you have to take responsibility as a parent and say, Okay, something is wrong here –

SHELLY. *(near tears)* You think I haven't asked myself a thousand times? What I could have – *should* have – done differently? Of course you try to protect kids from themselves, you try to guide them, you live your life a certain way to set an example, but at the same time children are not these little puppets. They come into this world with their own will, their own ideas, and Remy's been headstrong since should could talk. "My hand does it this way." That's what she told her kindergarten teacher who said she was making her fives backwards. "My hand does it this way."

JANINE. There were witnesses, girls who said they'd seen Remy, something in her bag. And when I tried to ask her –

REMY. These questions are *bigoted!* They're *offensive!*

SHELLY. And Remy just felt so betrayed. Patterson was the only place in the world she'd ever belonged, you know? I mean expelling her was just – I'll never forget it, she'd locked herself in her room, she was sobbing, I was leaning my forehead up against her door, just listening to my baby crying and I said, "Please, sweetheart, just come outside, let's talk about this, I know it's hard, I know what you're going through," And she bolted open the door and she looked at me and without saying a word she just –

(**REMY** *spits at* **SHELLY.**)

She spit on me.

(beat)

JANINE. I have a scar right here, the inside of my thumb. Because right after the fire I saw this little metal ornament on the floor, it had turned black. And for some reason I bent down to pick it up and – it was still hot. It burned me. I guess the shock...my reflexes... I barely felt it.

SHELLY. And I looked at her, standing there. She was out of breath. There was snot coming down her nose. And in her eyes there's this ferocious almost animal rage. It was just a moment like that. Then she slammed the door in my face.

(REMY *clicks off the lamp on her desk.* REMY *leaves her desk, walks upstage, her back to us. Beat.*)

LORI. I've always loved Christmas. The little white lights. All those fancy Christmas displays in the shop windows at Bergdorf's, the little reindeer. And really it has nothing to do with Jesus or God or anything it's just this wonderful time of year when everyone comes together and the city's all bustling and cozy. It's – beautiful. I think there ought to be a place for beauty in the world, I really do.

BERTA. Of course I don't envy Shelly. It's terrifying what a kid like that can get into over the internet. But a problem like this starts with the parents, I'm sorry, but it does. She could have taken any number of steps along the way.

SHELLY. That was the night she left.

LORI. My husband and I, we told Lindsey, we're not going to let this stand, she's worked too hard. We have meetings planned with the board, with the headmaster, we are fighting this, believe me. But she also knows people are talking. She knows what they're saying. And last night out of nowhere, she says to me, "Mommy, if Remy doesn't come back... How will I ever get past this?" And what am I supposed to say? This is not her fault.

SHELLY. (*holding a note*) The note says: "Escape is such a thankful word." (*nods*) Emily Dickinson. (*fighting tears*)

SHELLY. *(cont.)* She's so *smart.*

And then she writes: "Don't look for me. I'm sorry. Love, Remy."

JANINE. I wrote my dissertation on female adolescent psychology – allomaternal influences on teens and preteens in the context of environmental stressors. I call myself an expert and somehow... I don't know.

LORI. I've considered calling Shelly, I have, I just – don't know what I'd say.

JANINE. But maybe... Maybe I just – admired Remy. That's a silly thing to admit but – maybe that was my problem.

BERTA. The school paper ran a story this week. About the "alleged bullying." Like poor Remy would never have turned out the way she did if my daughter had been a better *friend.* Really? Is that fair? They printed Courtney's picture.

LORI. They published all five pages of Remy's "manifesto." I'd never actually read it.

JANINE. Right near the bottom it says: "The Truth About Christmas." That's the subheading, for the last part.

SHELLY. It's been two weeks.

She's fourteen years old.

*(Upstage, **REMY** turns to face out, walks to stand behind her desk.)*

JANINE. *(clears her throat, reads)* "The Truth About / Christmas."

BERTA & LORI. "The Truth About / Christmas..."

REMY. The truth about Christmas is that it's a time when more crimes are committed, more money is wasted, more pain is suffered than any other during the whole calendar year. Christmas means violence; Christmas means waste. Patterson should be smarter than to endorse the pervasive mythology of Hallmark, of Walmart, of Best Buy. Saying Christmas is a joyful time of year is just like saying high school is a joyful time of life. These white lies are toxic and deserve to be questioned.

(**REMY** *exits the stage.*)

SHELLY. And on the back of the note – because it's just this little ripped-off corner of something – on the back there's… I can't quite tell. But this is the part I haven't told anybody, not even my husband. Because it's something I don't recognize. Something with a molecule, something printed from a website. I mean I know Remy would never do anything to harm anyone. So it must be nothing. But I'm scared. Because I don't know. What it means.

JANINE. "These white lies are toxic. And deserve to be questioned."

SHELLY. All I know is I want her to come home.

Please. Just come home.

BERTA. Signed: "Remy McAllister…

LORI. Class of 2013."

SHELLY. Please.

Please.

(*Lights fade. End of play.*)

HANKSYLVANIA

By Travis Helwig

For Donna and Douglas Helwig

Hanksylvania was produced as part of the 36th Annual Samuel French Off Off Broadway Short Play Festival at the Lion Theater at Theater Row in New York City on July 19, 2011 and July 24, 2011 as part of the Festival Finals. It was directed by Emma Givens. The cast was as follows:

DEREK......................................Michael Antonucci

TANK.............................. Richard "Big Rich" Armstead

HANK..Jim Santangeli

LARSEN..Don Fanelli

CHARACTERS

HANK - 52. Coach. Fat, fat stomach. Graying.

LARSEN - 23. QB. Born a QB.

DEREK - 29. Place kicker. Wiry. A bit squeaky.

TANK - 30. Linebacker. Quiet but serious.

AUTHOR'S NOTE

Don't fuck it up.

ABOUT THE AUTHOR

Travis Helwig is writer, comedian and actor, who currently resides in Brooklyn, New York. A native of Stratford, Connecticut, he's a 2011 graduate of the MFA Dramatic Writing Program at the Tisch School of the Arts at New York University and one of the 2011 NYU nominees for the Kennedy Center MFA Playwrighting Prize. In 2008, his one-act play *A Breathless September* was performed by The George Washington University Department of Theater and Dance. In 2009, he directed his full-length play *Lots and Lots of Moss* for the Generic Theater Company in Washington, D.C., which won the 2009 Astere E. Claeyssens Prize. *The Huffington Post, Paste Magazine* and *Buzzfeed* called his parody Twitter account @FriendFromHS one of the "Best New Twitter Accounts of 2011." In *ELLE Magazine*, Ben McKenzie (the dude from *The O.C.*) called @FriendFromHS "pretty funny," so you know it's legit. He performs improv and sketch comedy around New York City. You can follow him @TravisHelwig.

(An NFL locker room. Meadowlands, New Jersey.)

(Fancy wooden lockers line the room.)

*(An oversized graying man, **HANK**, [52], paces in a loose baseball hat. His eyes are towards the ground as he breathes loudly. Sadly.)*

(He's also eating a sandwich.)

*(An entire football team enters, sweaty and disappointed. We see three members of the team: **LARSEN**, 23, skinny **DEREK**, 29, and **TANK**, a massive 31 year-old linebacker.)*

(After a few moments of silence, he speaks.)

HANK. I'm tired. I'm tired of you motherfuckers mucking around all willy-nilly. You understand me? I didn't come here to muck around and I sure as shit hope you didn't come here to muck around. Although it seems like everyone here woke up this morning and said 'you know what, I guess I'll forsake the millions of fucking dollars people pay me to win and just swing my dick around until the game's over.' You all say that this morning? Did you, Larsen?

LARSEN. No sir.

HANK. You sure about that?

LARSEN. Yes sir.

HANK. Then why did you spend the whole first half mucking around like a goddamn baby if you didn't come here to muck around?

LARSEN. They're blitzing every –

HANK. Larsen. I know muck. And that half was muck. You get paid millions of dollars. Earn it.

(He takes a bite of the sandwich.)

HANK. *(cont.)* Hey! Hey! Quick question! Who here plays professional football? Anyone? Anyone here play professional football?

*(**DEREK** and **TANK** raise their hands.)*

Put down your little baby hands. You're lying to me!

DEREK. Coach, they're seeing every play we call before we call it. I don't know how their doing it. We can't surprise them.

(a pause)

HANK. I looked at you for a moment and I said to myself, 'I don't know who that is.' But you're the kicker, right? The fucking place kicker wants to add something! And what a brilliant observation he's added! The other team must have the superhuman ability to read our minds. No, it can't be our fault. The other team is coached by David fucking Blaine!

LARSEN. Coach, he's right. We have to make some calls they aren't expecting. We practiced wildcat all week. They won't know how to handle that. Because, with all due respect, Coach, this isn't helping.

(He smiles, eats some more of the sandwich.)

HANK. Respect? You wanna know about respect? My father was a football coach. I watched him coach Namath. I watched him coach side by side with Ditka. I watched him win the Super Bowl. Three times. And I said, I want that man to know I can coach too. I want that man to respect me, not as a son, but as a coach. And he's dead now. And he's looking down from the bleachers in the sky and he's smiling. A big shit eating grin. And he's saying, 'Take a look, Jesus. My son is a big fat pussy. A big fat pussy who coaches a team of big fat pussy players who only win games when they happen to play against bigger and fatter pussies. Which doesn't happen very often, Jesus!" Okay, yeah QB, I'll respect you. Lets have a little chitchat. Let's learn each other. Tell me best buddy, what'd your father do for a living?

LARSEN. I'm just saying that we're working hard and if you insult us –

HANK. No, I'm serious Larsen. I wanna respect you. Tell me what your father did.

(beat)

LARSEN. He started in life insurance but ended up assistant coaching at Delaware.

HANK. A football family. What a surprise. Was he a good coach?

LARSEN. Better than most.

DEREK. My father was in make up.

HANK. Stop.

DEREK. Avon sir. Door to door.

HANK. Please stop.

DEREK. But he's no wimp. Coulda gone pro. He quit his senior year at Cal to become a gonzo journalist. But when he failed, my mom taught him to sell make up.

*(**HANK** is taken aback.)*

HANK. Your father's a brave man. Give up what he knows to pursue what he loves. Tank. Tell me about your father.

TANK. Never met him sir.

HANK. Your mother?

TANK. Never met her sir.

HANK. Holy christ, Tank. You're a raggamuffin?

TANK. Sir?

HANK. An Annie. A little orphan kid washing floors and getting slapped around and all that?

TANK. No sir. I was adopted by a minister when I was two months old.

HANK. A minister? Why ain't you a preacher?

TANK. My adopted father wanted me to play ball. So I played ball. I owed him that much.

HANK. Owed him? You didn't want to play ball?

TANK. Sir?

HANK. You didn't want to play football?

TANK. I'm a good football player.

HANK. That's not what I'm asking, Tank. Did you want to play football?

TANK. Well, I guess I did.

HANK. You sonuvabitch. What did you wanna be? Tell me.

TANK. Sir?

HANK. Instead of a football player. Tell me.

LARSEN. Coach, how is this helping? If we want to get back in this we need to start –

HANK. Shut up, we're making a break through. Go ahead Tank.

TANK. Well, I'm good at football. So maybe I was supposed to be a football player. But, I always wanted to work with dolphins. I love dolphins, Coach.

HANK. A fucking dolphin wrangler. Tank the dolphin wrangler.

LARSEN. We need to counter their five wide. If they're gonna play us that tight, I say we start driving it up their throats. And when they adjust – boom – wildcat. Real tricky shit. It's not over until it's over.

HANK. I wanted to be a conductor. Like on trains, you know? In my basement I had this big fucking train set with like a bridge and a fire station and all that bullshit. The train would go around the whole basement and back into the village. The thing was beautiful. I called it Hanksylvania. I would spend hours down there, just pretending to be the mayor, talking as the little people, with voices and all. *The citizens of Hanksylvania!* I'd have the little guys gossip about who might be having an affair and who came in on the last train that night and who shot the Sheriff's dog. I loved that.

LARSEN. Coach, seriously. We need to talk second half.

DEREK. Do you still have the train set?

HANK. No, no, no. As I got older my dad started to get worried, you know. Told my mother, rest her soul, that he wouldn't have his son be a fagg – excuse me, *homo* – playing with dolls all day. "Gotta get tough or else there's no future for him." I came back from school one day and the whole thing was gone. God, it was like a tiny 9/11. I can't remember another time I cried that hard. 'Cause it was mine, you know. I created it, and I chose what pieces went where, and no one else could tell me it was wrong or stupid or bad. Hanksylvania was mine. Then a couple weeks later I started peewee. Football's been my life since.

LARSEN. Great. Super. If you're not gonna lead this team –

TANK. I had an aquarium, sir. Like fish tanks. That's where I got my name.

HANK. Tank? Thought we called you that cause you're a large human being?

TANK. No sir. Fish tanks.

(**DEREK** *stands.*)

DEREK. I hate football. I don't like it. Even a little bit. I'm gonna stop playing football.

(**DEREK** *sits.*)

(**DEREK** *stands.*)

You guys always make fun of me, but I never wanted to be here. I hate it here. Football sucks.

(**DEREK** *sits.*)

HANK. I've been doing this for over thirty years. Thirty years and that kicker just said the most honest thing any one has ever said in a locker room.

LARSEN. HOW!? HOW IS THAT? I give you my heart every game. I put one hundred percent into everything I do. We sit in this room every Sunday and I pour my heart out for this team. I rally this team. Because I stand with my brothers on the field of battle. I bleed and I cry and I scream because of this team and this sport. We're here because we love each other. We're here because we love football.

HANK. No. I think I love trains. And trains are not gay, Larsen, if that's what you were thinking. Trains are pretty great. Football's... I don't know, it's just like...

DEREK. It gets sort of redundant.

TANK. Yeah, I get kinda bored.

HANK. It's boring, right! It's a boring thing to spend all of our time doing!

(A whistle blows off stage.)

LARSEN. I'm not gonna sit by and watch you destroy our chances for the second half. If you won't be a leader, I will. I'll call the plays. I'll dig in deep. And I'll lead this fucking team to glory even if I die doing it. What do you say boys?

(They look up at him quietly.)

What do you say boys?

*(**DEREK** shrugs a bit then –)*

DEREK. Thank you?

HANK. Larsen. Look at me. You *really* like football?

LARSEN. It's all I am.

HANK. Good for you. But it's not all I am. It's all my father was. I didn't choose this. And I don't really feel like playing anymore.

(another long whistle)

LARSEN. You can't quit the team at half-time.

HANK. Of course I can.

TANK. People are gonna be upset, Coach.

HANK. Fuck 'em. I'm a grown-ass man. Who cares what they say?

LARSEN. Don't turn your back on this game, Coach. What would your father say?

HANK. Fuck my father! And fuck football! And fuck Joe Namath! I don't wanna do this anymore! All I'm trying to say is...

(beat)

I don't know. Make up your own damn minds.

*(**HANK** leaves.)*

*(The sideline whistle blows twice. **HANK** responds:)*

HANK. *(offstage)* CHOO – CHOOOOOO!

(blackout)

MOUNTAIN SONG

by Josh Beerman

Mountain Song was produced as part of the 36th Annual Samuel French Off Off Broadway Short Play Festival at the Lion Theater at Theater Row in New York City on July 20, 2011 and July 24, 2011 as part of the Festival Finals. It was directed by Mark Cirnigliaro. The cast was as follows:

CHARLENE. . . . . Katie Lydic

ELIZABETH . . . . Laurie Dawn

TRISHA . . . . Christina Norris

CHARACTERS

ELIZABETH
CHARLENE
TRISHA

ABOUT THE AUTHOR

Josh Beerman is a playwright and director. His writing has been part of the FringeAct Festival of New Work at ACT Theater in Seattle, On the Table at Capitol Hill Arts Center, Theatre Schmeater's Northwest Playwrights Competition, and in their season. In New York he has had work produced for The Collective, Manhattan Repertory Theatre, and was part of the Samuel French Festival in 2010. Josh has worked in casting and assistant directing for Seattle Repertory Theatre and Artist Services for Brooklyn Academy of Music. He has his MFA from the New School for Drama class of 2011.

Morning

(The large kitchen of an old, tar roof, house in the mountains of North Carolina. Aged rotten pieces of wood create the outline of the room, like the foundation of an old house rotting from the inside out.)

(A radio plays music and sometimes weather news in the background.)

(There is a table in the middle of the kitchen. An urn rests in it's center.)

(Someone has been rolling dough for biscuits and stopped. There are vegetables cut. The feeling is that a large amount of food is in the middle of being prepared.)

*(A woman, in her mid-fifties, called **ELIZABETH**, kneels center stage scrubbing her floor. She is always cleaning. Something scurries in front of her and she squishes it. As she scrubs she talks with a thick Southern accent. She is alone but thinks she is talking to someone.)*

ELIZABETH. Older I get, easier it is to kill things. Use to not even kill bugs. Didn't like the idea. The feel. Like I would get myself caught up in some life cycle, what the heathen Asians call Karma. Always felt guilty bout it when I was young. Like something was coming back around. First I got square with killing bugs. Just a bug. An ant...or a beetle. You know the way a beetle feels when you step on it? Satisfying. Crunch. That sound. You know you kilt it cause of that sound. Know it's dead. Same with a chicken. Cept, your father use to use an ax, cut the head off, watch it run around for a minute fore it died. He'd laugh and laugh watching that chicken die. Not me. No ma'am. Too messy. Not satisfying. I just break the neck. That sound again. Like a beetle. Crunch. First time I did that I was standing outside, right outside this back door and that man, that husband of mine, he come out an laugh at me. He laughed cause I cried when I did it. I did too. Cried like a child. But not for the reasons he thought. Not cause I was weak. I cried cause I felt strong. Strong for the first time. I realized right there. Life was sacrifice. My whole life was everything for everyone else. And this...this idea of killing a small thing...it gave me control. Made me feel like more than I was. Made me a happier person. Anyway, from then on I always killed our supper. Never let him. Gave me something to be proud of on a daily basis. Now you got to find something to be proud of too. Here what I'm saying Charlene? You got to make your life here mean something. Cause there ain't nothing else out there for people like us. Like you. You hear me girl?

(She stops scrubbing.)

ELIZABETH. *(cont.)* Charlene. Charlene...

(She turns around but no one is there.)

(She looks to the urn. Silence.)

(CHARLENE, *a woman of eighteen or twenty, enters wiping her hands. She moves to the counter where she was making biscuits.)*

(CHARLENE *is what one might call simple.)*

CHARLENE. Temperature outside's dropping.

ELIZABETH. Where'd you go? I was talking to you.

CHARLENE. Porch. Get some more wood.

ELIZABETH. You wash your hands?

CHARLENE. Naw.

ELIZABETH. Why not?

CHARLENE. Ain't dirty.

ELIZABETH. You went out to the porch they are.

(She looks at her hands.)

CHARLENE. There ain't no dirt.

*(She shows **ELIZABETH** her hands.)*

ELIZABETH. We clean for germs, not for dirt.

CHARLENE. Germs?

ELIZABETH. Yes.

CHARLENE. What kind of germs?

ELIZABETH. Regular kind.

CHARLENE. Oh. Cause I couldn't see no germs.

ELIZABETH. Ain't about what you can see. This house was soiled with sickness.

*(**ELIZABETH** scrubs the floor harder.)*

Cannot keep this place clean. Always dirty. Seems like the more I clean more I find needs cleaning.

CHARLENE. Daddy always said –

ELIZABETH. How're them biscuits coming?

(moment)

CHARLENE. Good, Mama. Almost done with –

ELIZABETH. How many you making?

CHARLENE. Um, I dunno. I think we need bout...three dozen.

ELIZABETH. For how many people?

CHARLENE. Well, it's the whole congregation so –

ELIZABETH. Exactly. The whole congregation. That's at least...thirty people...and kids. Three dozen ain't enough. This is my house. People got to see my hospitality.

CHARLENE. Daddy always said –

ELIZABETH. Your daddy ain't here. This ain't his house no more. It's mine. Things are different now. You understand me?

CHARLENE. Yes, Ma'am.

*(The sound of foot steps on the creaky ceiling. Someone is walking on the floor above. **ELIZABETH** looks up, and watches the invisible person as they walk.)*

ELIZABETH. Why is your sister up in your daddy's sick room?

CHARLENE. Dunno.

(**ELIZABETH** *stares upward for a moment longer and goes back to scrubbing.*)

(*Someone says the word "ice" on the radio.*)

(*The phone rings. It is an old phone with a cord. Neither woman moves. A moment passes, more rings.* **CHARLENE** *looks up.*)

Mama.

ELIZABETH. What?

CHARLENE. You gonna get that?

ELIZABETH. Get what?

CHARLENE. The telephone.

ELIZABETH. Me? I am grieving.

CHARLENE. So.

ELIZABETH. One does not answer the phone in times of grief.

CHARLENE. I'm grieving too.

ELIZABETH. I am a grieving widow.

CHARLENE. I'm a grieving daughter.

ELIZABETH. Widow surpasses daughter in times of grief, and mother surpasses daughter all the time. Answer the phone.

CHARLENE. Yes, Ma'am.

(**CHARLENE** *cleans off her hands and answers the phone.*)

Hello. Hi, May Beth. Thank you. Best as can be. Sure.

(*She holds out the phone.*)

It's for you.

ELIZABETH. Who is it?

CHARLENE. What do you mean?

ELIZABETH. I cannot read minds.

CHARLENE. I said, "Hello, May Beth."

ELIZABETH. Oh it's May Beth. Gimmie that phone. Get back to them biscuits.

(*CHARLENE* hands the phone over. She goes back to her biscuits.)

Hello. Hi, May Beth. Thank you. You are sweet. Alright. Yes. Feels like he's still here. Walking around. Yes. So… them extra plates? Good. Whole congregation. I'll send Charlene round to get em. Thank you. Blessed to be surrounded. Amen. Thank you for helping. I have to finish the cleaning before guests get here. One must deal with what God puts forward. See you this afternoon. Bye bye now.

(*She hangs up the phone.*)

Great, bringing her biscuits. Woman bakes like she's preparing marble for a church floor. You need to go round to May Beth's and pick up her extra plates.

CHARLENE. By myself?

ELIZABETH. Yes by yourself.

CHARLENE. How many are there?

ELIZABETH. Many as you can carry.

(*CHARLENE* looks at *ELIZABETH.*)

What?

CHARLENE. Nothing.

(*ELIZABETH* goes back to cleaning.)

(*TRISHA* enters. A woman in her early-thirties, *TRISHA* is different, urban, and has almost no, if any accent. She carries a suitcase and wears her coat.)

ELIZABETH. Look who came down.

TRISHA. Hello.

(*ELIZABETH* notices the bag and coat.)

ELIZABETH. You leaving?

TRISHA. Soon.

ELIZABETH. Funeral in the morning, city in the evening.

TRISHA. Something like that.

ELIZABETH. One night? Can't be here for the reception?

TRISHA. Is that really what it's called?

ELIZABETH. Why? What you wanna call it?

TRISHA. Something else.

ELIZABETH. What's wrong with reception.

TRISHA. Too happy?

ELIZABETH. Ok…you staying for the food after the funeral?

TRISHA. I might.

ELIZABETH. Suit yourself.

TRISHA. News says there's a storm.

ELIZABETH. That's what it says.

TRISHA. Ice. Tends to make driving down the mountain dangerous.

ELIZABETH. You know, maybe *you should* get back there. Before ice comes. Get on the road soon. Don't you got work or something? What is it you do again?

TRISHA. You know what I do. You asked me yesterday.

ELIZABETH. Did I?

TRISHA. Yes.

ELIZABETH. Guess I forgot.

TRISHA. I'm a Paralegal.

ELIZABETH. I don't know bout that.

TRISHA. I work with lawyers.

(**ELIZABETH** *smiles and continues to clean in silence.*)

I was upstairs.

ELIZABETH. Heard you walking around. Figured it wasn't him.

TRISHA. Turned the corner in there and half of me thought he would still be in bed. Expected to see him taking turns. Pull on a cigarette, hit off an oxygen tank. Repeat as needed.

ELIZABETH. Damn things what killed him.

TRISHA. Put him in that bed. Burnt his lungs. Filled his heart. That's sure. I waited before I went in. Closed my eyes as I turned the corner. Sniffed for nicotine and vicks. Funny thing, I opened my eyes and got very cold. So I checked the windows for a draft. All fine. Thought, maybe it's the walls. A crack someplace. Old houses have cracks. But no. Nothing. Everything was where is should be, except him. But for some reason it was still freezing in there.

(ELIZABETH *stops and stares at* TRISHA.)

ELIZABETH. What you snooping for?

TRISHA. Wasn't snooping, just looking. *(moment)* I found all his medication.

(ELIZABETH *stares hard at* TRISHA.)

ELIZABETH. Did you now.

TRISHA. Yes. All of it. It's all there in his room. Full bottles. New, like he never took it.

ELIZABETH. You look around that room, you see it's clean now. Was dirty before he got sick. Dirty from when it was your room. Cleaned it myself. Spic and span.

TRISHA. You clean everything?

ELIZABETH. Everything 'cept his sheets. Got piles of his sheets to clean. Always dirty. Specially in there. That bed.

TRISHA. You do it all, don't you?

ELIZABETH. My house. Got to take care to keep things clean.

(moment)

CHARLENE. Oh God.

ELIZABETH. What?

(CHARLENE *hops up and down.*)

CHARLENE. Ummm…there's a cockroach.

ELIZABETH. What you think it's gonna do? Ask you to dance?

CHARLENE. I hate cockroaches.

ELIZABETH. Kill it.

CHARLENE. No.

ELIZABETH. Why not?

CHARLENE. Good Lord says –

(**ELIZABETH** *crushes the roach.*)

ELIZABETH. You got to grow a spine. That's what the good Lord says.

(**TRISHA** *smiles. It's forced. She puts her bag and coat down.*)

TRISHA. Can I help you with anything Charlene?

(**ELIZABETH** *stares hard at* **TRISHA**.)

ELIZABETH. She don't need your help.

CHARLENE. But –

ELIZABETH. Get back to work.

(*The phone rings again.*)

CHARLENE. Yes, Ma'am.

ELIZABETH. She's fine. Been doing this a long time. She doesn't need your help.

TRISHA. Maybe she –

ELIZABETH. (*to* **TRISHA**) No. She doesn't. Remember your place. Daddy's girl. That's what you are.

CHARLENE. You want me to get the –

ELIZABETH. No. I'll get it.

CHARLENE. I thought –

ELIZABETH. Changed my mind.

(**ELIZABETH** *goes to the phone and answers.*)

Hello. Hello? Anyone there? Hello? Who is that?

(*No one replies. She slowly hangs up. Something has unnerved her.*)

Need to see to cleaning the rest of my house.

(*She exits.* **CHARLENE** *starts to sing, she steps off stage. The light changes. She returns with a stack of plates. She is still singing.*)

Mid-morning

(**CHARLENE** *puts the plates down and returns to cooking. Music plays on the radio.* **CHARLENE***'s song from before bleeds into this scene.*)

(**TRISHA** *enters and listens to her sister.* **TRISHA** *starts to sing along.* **CHARLENE** *turns and smiles. The singing gets louder. They remember something nice of their childhood as they sing.*)

TRISHA. You still have such a nice voice.

CHARLENE. Sing every week.

TRISHA. Church choir?

CHARLENE. Yeah.

TRISHA. That's good. Can I help with anything?

CHARLENE. That's alright.

TRISHA. Come on.

CHARLENE. I'm fine.

TRISHA. Really.

CHARLENE. No.

TRISHA. I want to help.

CHARLENE. *(snapping)* I don't need help. Been doing this along time by myself.

(moment)

TRISHA. Sorry.

CHARLENE. It's alright. I shouldn't a… The day, that's all. She's got me doing all the cooking.

TRISHA. It's ok.

CHARLENE. You really want to help?

TRISHA. Yes.

CHARLENE. Mama said we need more biscuits. You can start getting them ones there on the pan while I make more dough.

TRISHA. Ok.

(As **CHARLENE** *starts to mix dough* **TRISHA** *looks around the kitchen for something. She finds a small mason jar and brings it over to the counter where the dough and pans are. She uses the mason jar to cut each biscuit from the dough.)*

*(***CHARLENE*** giggles at* **TRISHA***.)*

TRISHA. What?

CHARLENE. That's how I like to do it.

TRISHA. We have something in common.

CHARLENE. Yeah. Mama hates it.

TRISHA. We don't have to tell her.

CHARLENE. She'll see em when they're done.

TRISHA. Tell her I did it.

CHARLENE. Don't want you in trouble.

TRISHA. I won't get in trouble.

CHARLENE. Mama likes em drop style. No shape. Just plops dough on the pan. She also says it makes a mess of her canning jars. She gotta clean the dough off the rim. I think it's funny since now she's cleaning all the time anyway. What's a little biscuit off some glass? Anyhow, she don't believe in round biscuits.

TRISHA. Well…I do. I like a good round biscuit.

*(***TRISHA*** smiles at* **CHARLENE***. They work quietly.)*

CHARLENE. This is nice.

TRISHA. What's that?

CHARLENE. Just cooking with you. You remember we would sit on the porch everyday in the Summer while Mama cooked dinner and we'd wait for Daddy to come home.

TRISHA. Yes. You remember that?

CHARLENE. I do.

TRISHA. You were…what, five?

CHARLENE. I remember lots.

TRISHA. Remember what we did on the porch?

CHARLENE. Caught June bugs.

TRISHA. That's right.

CHARLENE. Find six or seven, tie em to strings, let em fly around us.

TRISHA. Like flying emeralds.

CHARLENE. I yusta like bugs. Now they make me creepy crawly.

TRISHA. It's different when you're young.

CHARLENE. I guess.

TRISHA. You're not scared of things cause you don't know any better.

CHARLENE. I had the most fun then. When you were still here. I'm the same age as when you left now.

TRISHA. I was young.

CHARLENE. I was only six. Eighteen now. A woman. Ain't an annoying little girl no more. So you could come back here. Don't have to worry about taking care of me now. I'm grown.

TRISHA. Do you think I left cause I took care of you?

CHARLENE. Didn't you?

TRISHA. No. Not at all.

CHARLENE. Oh. Always felt you did.

TRISHA. No. That's just what happens when you get old. You leave.

CHARLENE. You leave, you can come back. Don't have to live here. Near Mama. I know how she is. But we could see each other. Be close. Town's only twenty minutes.

TRISHA. I can't come back.

CHARLENE. Why?

TRISHA. I have a very full life.

CHARLENE. So if you didn't leave 'cause of me, then why'd you go?

TRISHA. School. I left to go to school.

CHARLENE. Naw. That don't seem right.

TRISHA. Not right?

CHARLENE. Not true.

TRISHA. You think it's not true?

CHARLENE. Might be true, but it ain't right.

TRISHA. What do you mean?

CHARLENE. I don't know. Like I got cobwebs and dust in the back a my head I can't see through. Some days I see there's something missing that makes more sense than what's here. Like a hush where words should be. Everything gets quiet and I hear corners whisper.

TRISHA. What do they say?

CHARLENE. Something's missing.

TRISHA. That's all?

CHARLENE. I guess.

TRISHA. Do they say you should do anything about it?

CHARLENE. What do you mean?

TRISHA. Try something new.

CHARLENE. I don't know.

TRISHA. Well, do you like to try new things?

CHARLENE. I guess. If they taste good.

TRISHA. Right, if they taste good. Me too.

CHARLENE. If it taste good I'll try it.

TRISHA. I think I know something that would taste real good.

(**ELIZABETH** *is about to enter but stops short to listen.*)

CHARLENE. What?

TRISHA. If you come live with me.

CHARLENE. What?

TRISHA. Come live with me.

CHARLENE. I can't go to the city.

TRISHA. You'd like it.

CHARLENE. What about mama?

TRISHA. She'd be fine.

CHARLENE. No kin there but you. I gotta to be around my people.

TRISHA. You'll find new people.

CHARLENE. There ain't nothing else out there for people like us

TRISHA. I have an extra bedroom, that could be all yours.

CHARLENE. I got a bedroom here.

TRISHA. You could have your own life there. Different kinds of people. You can step out the front door and go any place you want.

CHARLENE. I'd be scared living there. Mama says awful things happen in the city.

TRISHA. Awful things happen everywhere, even here. I'll tell you a secret.

CHARLENE. What?

TRISHA. Daddy told me bad things would happen here if you stayed.

CHARLENE. He did not.

TRISHA. He did. Said he wanted you to live someplace else. Said he was worried.

CHARLENE. Bout what?

TRISHA. Said Mama didn't take good care of you.

CHARLENE. I don't believe that. When did you talk to Daddy?

TRISHA. He wrote me letters.

CHARLENE. He wrote you letters? Never said nothing to me. Hardly talked.

TRISHA. He'd want you to leave. There are bad things here Charlene. You say you're grown but look how she treats you. I'd take care of you and let you be anything you want.

(**TRISHA** *finishes cutting the biscuits and slides them in the oven. Then she stands for a moment in contemplation.*)

CHARLENE. Tell me something else great that's in the city.

TRISHA. Me. I'm there.

Mid-day

(**CHARLENE** *is placing biscuits on a plate while* **ELIZABETH** *puts plates out for company.* **CHARLENE** *notices the quiet hanging over the room.*)

CHARLENE. Mama.

ELIZABETH. Hm?

CHARLENE. You ok?

ELIZABETH. Fine.

CHARLENE. You sure?

ELIZABETH. Yes.

CHARLENE. Ok.

(*They go back to working.*)

CHARLENE. You sure cause –

ELIZABETH. Lord girl. Yes. I'm fine. Just thinking.

CHARLENE. Bout what?

ELIZABETH. Goodness.

CHARLENE. What you mean?

ELIZABETH. Would you say I'm good to you?

CHARLENE. Yes, Ma'am.

ELIZABETH. I find that hard to believe.

CHARLENE. Why?

ELIZABETH. Back when I had your sister in my belly. After a real bad winter, your daddy took me out to collect logs. 'Cause of the ice and snow storms, the trees all break. He'd chop em up and we'd store em for next winter. Wood for the stove to heat the house. It's just spring and we was out there, collecting logs. Him cutting, me carrying one or two, wobbling to the truck all pregnant, and I turn around and he's just staring at me. I say, "What?" "Why you staring at me for?" He said "You look pretty." Swear, I turned the color of a red delicious apple. No one ever said such a thing to me.

CHARLENE. I can't hardly believe my daddy said that.

ELIZABETH. And that was nicest thing he *ever* said to me.

CHARLENE. Ever?

ELIZABETH. Yeah. 'Cause after your sister was born he only had eyes for her. Nothing for me but silence and a stare. I couldn't never make that man smile, but I was good to him. Your sister though, he smiled for her like she was sunshine in Spring.

CHARLENE. Why're you telling me –

ELIZABETH. I'm making a point.

(a moment)

Your sister will make you smile. Fill you up, but in the end, she's like her daddy, just stare at you saying nothing. Not like me.

(CHARLENE stares guiltily at her mother.)

You think there's something else out there for you?

(moment)

CHARLENE. I don't know.

ELIZABETH. You wanna find out?

(moment)

CHARLENE. Maybe.

ELIZABETH. You know what it is makes me good?

CHARLENE. What?

ELIZABETH. I tell you the way things are. You can't even kill a cockroach. How you gonna go to a city? There ain't nothing there for a slow-witted girl like you. You think about that and remember, your sister is a wind done blown.

(ELIZABETH leaves CHARLENE alone.)

CHARLENE. Yes, Ma'am.

Later that day

(The radio plays music. **TRISHA** *sings along to it. "I'll Fly Away" or some other gospel mountain tune.* **TRISHA** *is alone in the kitchen. She stares at the urn. The table is set for company. Lots of plates, and food.)*

*(***ELIZABETH*** *enters.)*

TRISHA. Hey.

ELIZABETH. Hey yourself.

TRISHA. Still cleaning?

ELIZABETH. Always. This house –

TRISHA. Is always dirty. I know. Germs.

ELIZABETH. Yeah well…

TRISHA. You can't clean everything. Something's don't go away.

ELIZABETH. You see something needs taking care of?

TRISHA. Maybe. Yeah.

ELIZABETH. Tell me where it is. I'll clean it.

TRISHA. Up in his room. The sheets are still piled. The bed…

ELIZABETH. What? Say it.

(moment)

TRISHA. Think I'm gonna go before people get here.

ELIZABETH. Are you?

TRISHA. Yeah.

ELIZABETH. Don't want to see your cousins and such?

TRISHA. Saw 'em at the funeral.

ELIZABETH. Had enough.

TRISHA. Just don't feel like family anymore.

ELIZABETH. I see. Your…sister?

TRISHA. Yes?

ELIZABETH. Gonna say goodbye?

TRISHA. Maybe.

ELIZABETH. Can't decide?

(The phone starts to ring.)

TRISHA. No. That's up to her.

(moment)

ELIZABETH. Damn that thing. Ringing all day.

TRISHA. I'll get it.

ELIZABETH. Leave it.

TRISHA. But –

ELIZABETH. I said leave it. Let it ring.

TRISHA. Fine.

(They both stare at the phone. It won't stop ringing.)

(Finally **ELIZABETH** *answers.)*

ELIZABETH. Hello.

(silence)

Hello. Who is this? What do you want? Say something. Say something.

(She hangs up.)

Son of a bitch. Like he's calling me. Like he's still…

TRISHA. Who?

(Moment. Silence.)

ELIZABETH. Nobody. She won't go.

TRISHA. It's up to her.

ELIZABETH. Why would you take her from here?

TRISHA. I'm not taking her. She wants to go.

ELIZABETH. So now, after all this time you can decide what's right for her?

TRISHA. I know what you did, I'll tell her.

*(***ELIZABETH*** laughs.)*

ELIZABETH. Oh really? No, I don't think so. I tell you though. At the end he just laid there looking through me. I'd ask if he was in pain, he'd just turn away. He's disappointed it was me. I just wanted to know if he was in pain. That's all. If I could help. If he needed me. Nothing. He'd say nothing. Just that cold look. Made me so angry. One day he's staring, and I'm smiling, being good, talking to him as usual, making his bed, cleaning him, wiping him, feeding him and I decide I had enough. If you don't talk then I don't know what's wrong and If I don't know what's wrong then you don't get my help. And I told him that. To his face. Yeah, I stopped giving him his medicine. From there, was a week afore he died. I was there. And you know what that son of a bitch did right at the end? He smiled. He did. And this sound came out of him. This sound like something inside being crushed. His breath made a cracking noise, his broken heart stopped, and he disappeared. I knew it was over cause a choice I'd made. I did something 'cause a you. 'Cause he always loved you. Since you were a little girl. I realized every time he opened his eyes and saw me, he wished it was you. It was never him I should a been angry at. You took him from me, not sickness. Or maybe the sickness was you. So now you know what I did, but it don't mean nothing. 'Cause what's worse, what I did or what you are?

TRISHA. I loved him.

ELIZABETH. Too much.

TRISHA. I couldn't help it.

ELIZABETH. He's your daddy.

TRISHA. I couldn't be his daughter.

ELIZABETH. And now you can't be anything to anyone can you. He ruined you.

TRISHA. No. This is about you. You're just afraid of –

ELIZABETH. Being without Charlene? That's what you think. I ain't. I ain't afraid. You are. You're all alone in this world. You really think you can just come in here, take her away, and never tell her the truth.

TRISHA. What?

ELIZABETH. I was the prettiest of his cousins. And I knew I'd be his wife someday. That's when we was kids. What'd you think you'd be?

(Moment. **TRISHA** *is speechless.)*

Got more in common, you and I. Both loved him, and both had one of his children. You try to take her, I tell her she's your daughter and she will be destroyed.

TRISHA. Why would you do that?

ELIZABETH. You never did listen. If not for you'd he'd a loved me.

TRISHA. I'm your daughter.

*(***CHARLENE*** enters wearing a nice dress.)*

CHARLENE. Yall ain't dressed.

(Both women look at her. Silence.)

TRISHA. I have to go.

CHARLENE. Now?

TRISHA. Yes. I have to leave.

CHARLENE. I thought…you ain't gonna stay till after?

TRISHA. No. I can't. Storm.

CHARLENE. So stay till it's over. I been thinking –

TRISHA. Can't.

*(***TRISHA*** picks up her suitcase and coat.)*

I should go now. If I don't go I have to wait till tomorrow. And tomorrow everything will be all covered with ice. Supposed to be a big storm. If I go now I'll miss it. If not trees break, cover the roads, and block traffic. Same trees Daddy used to take me to the woods to collect in Spring. We'd collect logs all day. He'd stare at me and smile…tell me how pretty I was.

(The phone begins to ring.)

CHARLENE. Why are you going?

TRISHA. Can't wait that long. Can't wait for things to melt.

(**CHARLENE** *is broken-hearted by her sister.* **TRISHA** *slowly, quietly picks up her suitcase, puts on her coat and leaves.* **CHARLENE** *does not watch her go.* **ELIZABETH** *does.*)

ELIZABETH. Wish I had more time to clean 'fore people arrive. This house is always dirty.

(**ELIZABETH** *answers the phone.*)

Hello...hello? I know it's you. You want to haunt me? Go right ahead old man. I can hold out till death. You made me strong.

(**CHARLENE**, *upset, starts to go but stops, looking down stage at something.*)

And when I die, I'm a find a way to haunt your ghost. And won't that be something, me haunting you after you're dead.

(*A cockroach scurries across the floor.* **CHARLENE** *takes a step and lays her foot on top of it. A cracking sound is heard.* **ELIZABETH** *sees this and smiles.*)

(*blackout*)

PLUCK & TENACITY

a short
game-changer
revolution
rupture
spit-and-run
break-up
from this day forth grossly altered
play

by Daniella Shoshan

Pluck & Tenacity was produced as part of the 36th Annual Samuel French Off Off Broadway Short Play Festival at the Lion Theater at Theater Row in New York City on July 21, 2011 and July 24, 2011 as part of the Festival Finals. It was directed by Colette Robert. The cast was as follows:

PLUCK.................................... Jon-Michael Reese

TENACITY.......................................Sheldon Best

A Crew of Two:

PLUCK,
a shy, deep-feeling brotha, ripe ol' age a' Fifth Grade.
if they're a sandwich, he's the gushy grape jelly.
if they're a school field trip, he's the planetarium ceiling.
if they're a hoodie, he's the heart on its sleeve.

and his best friend

TENACITY,
a fiery Fifth Grader with a swagger and a side-smile.
if they're a sandwich, he's the bread, the crunchy pb and the knife that cuts it on a diagonal.
if they're a school field trip, he's the stolen fossil showed-off in the bus back seat.
if they're a hoodie, he's the zipper.

ABOUT THE AUTHOR

Daniella Shoshan is a New York (formerly of New Jersey) playwright. Recent projects include: *Jack Perry is Alive (And Dating)* (NYMF 2011); *An Improvised Explosive Device: an MTV war story* (FringeNYC 2011); *Pluck & Tenacity* (winner, Samuel French OOB Festival 2011); *Yes We Can* (Down Payment Productions, Walkerspace); *Ya Heard Me* (SFOOB 2010); *They Call Him Young Lou* (MFA Thesis Productions, The Cherry Pit). MFA: Columbia University, 2010; BFA: NYU, 2006. She has been mentored by Kia Corthron and Stephen Adly Guirgis. She bakes crazy delicious cookies.

(A young kid on the block. Sits on the stoop.)

(Craning his neck up at an unseen fire escape, an unseen window.)

(He sings, sort of low, but sweet. Like, the song is for someone…)

*(His name is **PLUCK**.)*

PLUCK. *(singing)*
SUMMER ON MY FRONT STEPS,
DAMN IT'S HOT.
HARD TO KEEP MY COOL, 'CAUSE
I LIKE YOU A LOT.
SO SWEET SO FINE I GOTTA MAKE YOU MINE.
YOU BEEN WHIRLIN' ROUND MY MIND LIKE A HULA HOOP
GIRL YOU STIR MY SOUL LIKE ICE CREAM SOUP.

(Another kid appears. Same age as Pluck.)

*(His name is **TENACITY**.)*

*(And he is pissed, man. He gets up in **PLUCK**'s grill.)*

TENACITY. *(a combination of rage and disbelief)*
Was that a…?
Did I just…
Hold up.
Were you *singing*?

PLUCK. …Yes.

TENACITY. Are you out here singing…a *love song*?

PLUCK. …Yes.

TENACITY. Have you been…
Have you been right here? Singing? A LOVE SONG?

PLUCK. Yes.

TENACITY. For four days?

PLUCK. Has it been four days?

TENACITY. I been looking for you for four days.

PLUCK. Don't feel like four days.

TENACITY. I thought you were writing. I thought, all this time, you were working on lyrics.

PLUCK. For four days?

TENACITY. Yes.

PLUCK. ...That's a long time to be writing.

TENACITY. I know.

PLUCK. I did write *some* lyrics.

TENACITY. Well a'ight, then.

PLUCK. But then I been out here singing them.

TENACITY. ...These are them? That was them?

PLUCK. Some of them.

TENACITY. This is what you've been working on.

PLUCK. Do you like it?

TENACITY. This love song?

PLUCK. Yes.

TENACITY. No. I fucking hate it.

PLUCK. I think it really says something.

TENACITY. Four days, really? *This?*

PLUCK. I got another verse, you only heard the first –

TENACITY. You musta gone crazy. When's the last time you ate a bite?

PLUCK. Don't care.

TENACITY. *(low whisper)* How you gonna take a poo out here?

PLUCK. Don't matter.

TENACITY. It matters. Shit matters. Shit besides this.

PLUCK. Nothing matters besides this.

> *(beat)*

TENACITY. So you forgot our oath, 's'what you're telling me.

PLUCK. I didn't forget our oath.

TENACITY. Since kindergarten, we've held that oath, man. Been the plan since goddamn sandboxes and snack-time. You remember the fruit-roll up oath, don't you?

PLUCK. I remember it, T.

TENACITY. Swore it over fruit-roll ups. That's how holy, that's how serious business we were.

PLUCK. I said I remember it.

TENACITY. Used to be hella weird with your roll-ups, too, man. Used to dip yours in ketchup and I never even told a soul about that gross shit.

PLUCK. I grew outta that.

TENACITY. You grow outta our oath?

PLUCK. No.

TENACITY. Prove it to me, then. What did we swear to do?

PLUCK. *(sighs; reluctantly recites)* To flip the script on the rap game and revolutionize what hip-hop represents on a global scale.

TENACITY. A *global* scale?

PLUCK. A universal scale of unstoppable magnitude.

TENACITY. That's right. Now, you feel you doing that by sitting out here singing the least gangsta song I ever heard?

PLUCK. I already told you I ain't a gangsta. I'm a Romeo.

TENACITY. And I already told you *I'll* be the gangsta, you can be a Romeo, just as long as your bleeding heart is gushing sick lyrics over a skull-busting track. 'Cause that's what you are to this group, Pluck – the heart.

PLUCK. If I'm the heart, what are you?

TENACITY. The….jaws. And like, the venom.

(Beat. **PLUCK** *looks at* **TENACITY** *skeptically.)*

TENACITY. Look, we're a team; I'm the aggression, you're the seduction.

PLUCK. I'm trying to seduce the girl of my dreams right now –

TENACITY. Wait, hold up, that was kinda sexy.

(He raps.)

I BRING THE HARDCORE, YOU BRING THE CLASSY;
YOU MISTER SWEET P, I'M DOWNRIGHT T-NASTY.
YOU SUPPLY THE HOPE – PLAYA, I'LL SUPPLY THE HOW-TO;
YOU LOOKIN' FOR LOVE, SHIT,

(He unzips his fly.)

I'LL GIVE IT YOU NOW, BOO –

PLUCK. HEY! HEY! Back up, Tenacity! That's too much, man.

TENACITY. *(recovering; re-zipping)* Sorry, I got caught up in myself.

PLUCK. This – me and her? – this ain't about that, ok?

TENACITY. What's it about, then, huh?

PLUCK. It's about…

(He sings up to her.)

I WANT TO CALL YOU UP,
TALK FOR HOURS,
SHOW UP AT YOUR MAMMA'S HOUSE
RING YOUR BELL WITH FLOWERS;
WANT YOU TO FEEL JOY KNOWIN' I'M YOUR BOY –

TENACITY. *(tries to add a rap to Pluck's song)*
YEEEEAAAAHHH BOYYY,
I'LL BE YOUR CHEW TOY, YOU BE MY BARBIE DOLL;
I'LL TIE YOU UP WITH YOUR JUMP ROPE, SLAM YOU 'GAINST THE –

PLUCK. Stop, man, stop. You're messing this up.

TENACITY. I don't mess shit up, I enhance it.

PLUCK. Not this. This is a solo track.

TENACITY. A what?

PLUCK. This one's just me.

TENACITY. Just you? You're telling me there's no room on this joint for me, your partner, your best friend? I can't even, like…come in on the remix or something?

*(**PLUCK** shakes his head, nope.)*

TENACITY. *(cont.)* You can't have a hit on your own, you need some power behind you. I'm your ammo.

PLUCK. I don't wanna write war, I wanna write love.

TENACITY. Fuck love. Love don't make a rap-album dynasty. Content like that'll get you nowhere fast, son. This girl's not worth a slow-jam, she never cared you like her. You can tell a knock-knock so good it could slit a throat but has she ever laughed at your jokes, or seen how sweet and sensitive you are? *(up to the window)* WHAT'S A' MATTER, YOU DON'T LIKE JOKES?

PLUCK. But I've loved her since the fourth grade, T.

TENACITY. We're only in Fifth grade now, Pluck.

PLUCK. I been lovin' her for 365 days in 365 ways. 5 school days a week and twice as much on weekends. I can't see how's life worth livin' if I don't got this girl on my arm.

TENACITY. Lemme ask you – you can see how's life worth living with a high-ass voice and a two-dollar allowance? 'Cause we haven't hit puberty yet and you've never seen currency over a ten dollar bill, so I'd say you got a lots still left to live for. And if you need more reasons, I'll give 'em to you – 1. FuBu 2. Phat Farm 3. The new LL Cool J collection now available at Sears 4. Nike. 5. A Hummer. 6. Goldfish swimming in the headrests of that Hummer. Or clown fish. Like Nemo. Do you read me?

PLUCK. That's all you want, man? You wouldn't even miss me rapping with you, it's all just about the clothes and the car? You don't need me for any of that. All's I'd be is someone to remember to feed the fish.

TENACITY. *(considers this)* …I do kill mad fish.

PLUCK. I know. 'Cause you're straight selfish, T. You're not asking me to leave this stoop for us, you're asking for me to leave for *you* and your closet and your stupid superficials. But for me?

(He turns to sing.)

MORE THAN BLING, FINE THINGS OR A PIMPED-OUT COUP –
I JUST WANT YOU TO SPOON ME LIKE ICE CREAM SOUP.

(**TENACITY** *clamps his hand on* **PLUCK**'*s mouth.*)

TENACITY. That's enough. I can't hear that R&B crooning from you, Pluck. It hurts my…my…

(**PLUCK** *puts a hand on* **TENACITY**'*s shoulder.*)

PLUCK. *(quietly)* I don't want to hurt your feelings, Tenacity.

TENACITY. Fuck feelings, I don't have feelings, I was gonna say it hurts my hip-hop sensibilities. My Lil Wayne brain. My Jay-Z spleen and my Notorious gut. And I'm gonna tell you what, Pluck. You want to sing love songs. You want to sing them solo? I'm voting you out the group.

(beat)

How you like that soup?

(beat)

I got a recording studio lined up and everything. I'll make our demo without you.

PLUCK. How? With who?

TENACITY. Your brother.

PLUCK. Lil' Ego?

TENACITY. You know it.

PLUCK. How're you gonna replace me with my little brother?

TENACITY. Easy. He built a studio in your garage.

PLUCK. He can't do that, he's eight-years old! And you said yourself I been out here four days – you can't build a studio in four days.

TENACITY. Well he did, he's all industry, he's three-feet nine inches of know-how and do-now and guess what, he's my new collaborator. We're gonna get our demo made in the shade drinking lemonade. Or Crystal. 'Cause that's fancier.

PLUCK. You can't drink Crystal and get rich and fancy without me, Tenacity. You said I'm the heart.

TENACITY. Looks like I got myself a heart transplant, then.

PLUCK. So that's it. You're gonna trade me in for my little brother?

TENACITY. *(pointing up at the window)* You're gonna trade me in for her? For this big impossible? 'Cause you and me making a name for ourselves, that's only a small impossible, that we can chase.

(a moment)

(They turn away from each other, considering.)

Are we gonna be an empire? Are we're gonna ride in side-by-side thrones in the hummer of our shared fantasy, or…

PLUCK. …Or?

TENACITY. …Or am I gonna go record a multi-platinum album in your garage without you and then when I see you at school, if I see you at school, I'm gonna just nod a little and be like, *hey, P,* and maybe you'll like sorta wave and look away and be like, *yeah, uh, what's up, T,* and then it'll be like we never even had nothing between us.

(beat)

*(***PLUCK*** looks up at the fire escape.)*

PLUCK. I guess…I guess I'll just see you in school, maybe.

(beat)

TENACITY. A'ight.

PLUCK. A'ight.

*(***TENACITY*** slowly walks away, as **PLUCK** watches him go.)*

(beat)

*(***PLUCK*** stands, gathers his courage, calls up to the window.)*

Girl. Oh, Girl.

Damn, girl.

I been standing out here…

Man, feels like a long time slash no time at all.

PLUCK. *(cont.)* You feel me?

    'Cause that's what you do to me.

    Get me all...

    Confused.

    'Cept for one thing.

    One thing I know for true.

    One thing I ain't mixed up about at all.

    You know what that is?

    Lend me an ear, girl.

    And I'll tell you about it.

    (He's about to sing, when **TENACITY** *rushes back on, pushing in front of* **PLUCK***.)*

TENACITY. *(rapping)*

    BABY, YOU HEARD ALOOF FROM THIS GOOF

    MAKIN' YOU MUSHY GUSHY PROMISES

    YOU LIKE A SHY GUY, FINE,

    I'LL SHOW YOU WHAT MY MODEST IS:

    MY BOY'S PUPPY LOVE IS WHACK

    LET ME THROW YOUR ASS A DOG BONE

    I CAN UPGRADE YOUR LOVE DESSERT

    FROM A 'CHIPWHICH TO A KING CONE

    (strikes a pose; then, as an afterthought, adds)

Wanna come chill in my recording studio? Got a bicycle and some juiceboxes up in there, too.

(A moment. **PLUCK** *stands there, a combination of rage and disbelief.)*

(Then, something happens between them: in their faces, their bodies that reveals that this mythical girl, this object of their affection/conflict has chosen Tenacity.)

(He starts to triumphantly swagger off.)

(But pauses, looking almost sheepishly at the dejected **PLUCK***.)*

See what you made me do, Pluck? If you're not with me...Gots to turn my rap-dagger upon thee, man.

(He exits.)

(PLUCK *stands alone for a moment, before he plops back down onto the stoop.)*

PLUCK. *(singing glumly)*
TOOK HOLD A' MY HEART IN ONE FELL SWOOP;
THEN LEFT ME IN A PUDDLE LIKE ICE CREAM SOUP.

(Lights fade on the stoop.)

End of Play

MY NAME IS YIN

by Tom Swift

My Name Is Yin was originally developed by PlayGround (James A. Kleinman, Artistic Director) for the Monday Night PlayGround reading series in residence at Berkeley Repertory Theatre on November 17, 2003. It was directed by James A. Kleinman. The cast was as follows:

THE BEAR	Kerri Shawn
THE WRITER	Jason Frazier
ALF KJAELLSTROEM	Lizzie Calogero
THE HUSBAND	Brian Herndon
THE WIFE	Tina Marie Murray
THE AUDIENCE MEMBER	Caroline Doyle

My Name Is Yin was premiered by PlayGround at the 8th Annual Best of PlayGround Festival (2004) on June 12, 2004. It was directed by James A. Kleinman. The cast was a follows:

THE BEAR	Kerri Shawn
THE WRITER	Mark Rafael Truitt
ALF KJAELLSTROEM	Gwen Loeb
THE HUSBAND	Gabriel Marin
THE WIFE	Julia McNeal
THE AUDIENCE MEMBER	Sam Misner

My Name Is Yin was produced by Tom Swift and His Amazing Productions, LLC, at the Lion Theater at Theater Row on July 23, 2011 and July 24, 2011. It was directed by Christopher Mirto, with costumes by Ana Milosevic. The cast was as follows:

THE BEAR	Lisa Birnbaum
THE WRITER	Tony Torn
ALF KJAELLSTROEM	Jason Martin
THE HUSBAND	Jay Smith
THE WIFE	Juliana Francis Kelly
THE AUDIENCE MEMBER	Lisa Kitchens
THE ARTISTIC DIRECTOR	Christopher Mirto

CHARACTERS

THE BEAR - An American Brown Bear, female

THE WRITER - A journalist, male

THE AUDIENCE MEMBER - An outspoken older woman

ALF KJAELLSTROEM - A Swedish Provincial Spokesman with a German accent, male

THE HUSBAND - A man

THE WIFE - A woman

THE ARTISTIC DIRECTOR - An Artistic Director, male

SETTING

An empty stage with several pairs of shoes strategically placed. The shoes can be filled with butter, but this is not necessary. There may also be a writer's desk or table, with computer or notepad, downstage right, but this is not necessary either.

AUTHOR'S NOTES

Pronunciations:

Kjaellstroem	KELL-strum
Jämtland	YEMPT-land
Yu Xiuzhen	yoo ZHOO-zhen

CHOICES

THE ARTISTIC DIRECTOR is optional, and can be cut, if necessary. If that choice is made, simply string together **THE WRITER**'s lines in that section.

The final gun-shot can also be cut (when **THE WRITER** drops the gun). Alternatively, after that gun-shot, a body can fall from the lighting booth.

THE AUDIENCE MEMBER could wear a blood-pack, which explodes when she is shot, but this is not necessary. (No other 'blood-effects' should be used.)

Regarding staging, successful productions have played the opera section as written, or have jumped to the final line of the aria ("All'alba vincero!") and the rising orchestration which follows. Both have worked, and that's the key. There is only *one* direction for the end of the play: make it work.

One Final Note: If you aren't having fun in rehearsal, tech and performance, then you haven't figured out this play. So have fun, go big, add, subtract and enjoy.

ACCENTS

The only *required* accent is **ALF KJAELLSTROEM**'s – it must be German. **THE HUSBAND** and **THE WIFE** can have Swedish accents, or not (or one can have a Swedish accent, and the other, not). If **THE BEAR** has an accent, which is optional, consider a heavy Brooklyn or New York dialect.

CREDITS

ABOUT THE AUTHOR

Tom Swift is a playwright, producer and financial planner. He currently serves as Captain of the Financial Avengers®, a registered investment advisory firm that he co-founded with his side-kick, The Oracle. Together they recently founded a production company: Tom Swift and His Amazing Productions, LLC. He is a member of the PlayGround Writer's Pool and a four-time PlayGround Emerging Playwrights Award winner. He is currently working on a full-length gay marriage play *(A Marriage)*, a television concept (*The Financial Avengers News and Variety Hour*) and a book (*The Rules of the Financial Avengers: Winning the Fight for Financial Freedom in Post-Bubble America.*) Most recently in New York he served as Associate Producer for *Abraham Lincoln's Big Gay Dance Party*. He has a degree in acting from Northwestern University, is a member of the Dramatists Guild, and resides in Berkeley, California.

(THE BEAR enters, carrying shoes filled with butter. THE BEAR carefully places the shoes around the stage.)

THE BEAR. *(to the audience)* What are you looking at?

(THE BEAR exits. THE WRITER enters.)

THE WRITER. I am an artist.

(pause)

No, that's not right. I am a writer.

(THE BEAR enters with more shoes.)

No. I am a journalist. I'm just a journalist. I want to be an artist, but I'm just a journalist.

THE BEAR. To be clear, I am a bear. I am an American Brown Bear. Actually, that's not quite correct. I am an *expatriate* American Brown Bear.

(places shoes)

What? You've never seen a bear doing an installation before? That's why I left, you know. That is exactly why I left.

(exits)

THE WRITER. My most widely published work was a story I wrote about shoes filled with butter. It was picked up by the Associated Press. It ran all over the world. Millions read it.

(THE BEAR enters, with shoes.)

THE BEAR. No one was supposed to see this. I chose a remote location for a reason. It was a private installation. It was for her. And, me. Not for you. Everything you touch you destroy.

(exits)

THE WRITER. It felt good to be widely read. For once, I felt important.

(**ALF KJAELLSTROEM** *enters, wearing a uniform. He addresses the audience.*)

ALF KJAELLSTROEM. I am the Provincial Spokesman. I am also in charge of heavy equipment. I am a very important man.

(**THE BEAR** *enters with more shoes.*)

THE BEAR. This was never meant to be dangerous.

ALF KJAELLSTROEM. One day, I will be elected Prime Minister, and when I am, Sweden will be great again. Greater even than France!

(*Pause. He exits.*)

THE WRITER. The story takes place in Sweden.

THE BEAR. I came here to escape. To experiment. I know what you're thinking. You're thinking, "If she's an expatriate, why did she choose Sweden? Why not France?"

THE WRITER. It's why I'll never be a great artist. Sweden is not known for its art. Go ahead, name one great Swedish artist.

THE AUDIENCE MEMBER. August Strindberg.

THE WRITER. Dammit! Name another. Go on, name another. See? See?

THE BEAR. Let's just say the French are not *laissez faire* when it comes to granting visas to American Brown Bears.

THE WRITER. If I were French, I would probably be a great artist. You can name a lot of great French artists.

THE BEAR. The Swedes are much cooler when it comes to visas.

THE WRITER. Like Sartre,

THE BEAR. And, they have better fish.

THE WRITER. Ionesco –

THE AUDIENCE MEMBER. Can you *please* get started?

THE WRITER. Exposition is one of my problems. I just can't
– it just never – oh, God, my life is useless.

(*He cries.*)

Sorry. I'm sorry. From the AP News Wire: Stockholm,
Sweden, October 9th. "*Hikers Find 140 Shoes Filled With
Butter.* As shoe collections go, the one found by a pair
of Swedish hikers definitely had no place in any closet.
A Swedish couple hunting on a remote mountain
Sunday in Sweden's province of Jämtland found 70
pairs of shoes, all filled with butter."

THE HUSBAND (*offstage*) Hurry. We're almost there.

THE WIFE. I'm coming.

THE HUSBAND. (*Enters from house, carrying a rifle. He turns
and looks at the audience, using binoculars.*)
Ahhhhh! Look. Look. Just look at the view.

(**THE WIFE** *enters. She stops, abruptly, seeing the shoes.
She gasps.*)

THE WIFE. Oh.

(**THE BEAR** *looks at her.*)

THE HUSBAND. Isn't it breathtaking?

THE WIFE. (*walking among the shoes*) Oh, my. Oh, it's…won-
derful. I've never seen anything like it.

(*She cries, overwhelmed.*)

It redefines me.

THE HUSBAND. Let's hunt.

(**THE BEAR** *flees.*)

THE WIFE. I'll never kill again.

THE HUSBAND. You alright?

(*He turns and sees the shoes for the first time.*)

What the hell?

(*Startled, he trains the gun on the art installation.*)

THE WIFE. No, not hell. That's one interpretation, I suppose, but I don't see it. It's so much more.

THE HUSBAND. What – what is the meaning of this?

THE WIFE. Don't you see? Don't you see the meaning?

THE HUSBAND. Why are you crying?

THE WIFE. Who are you?

THE HUSBAND. Who am I? I'm your husband.

THE WIFE. No, you're not. You're a stranger.

THE HUSBAND. Elka –

THE WIFE. Don't call me that. That's not my name.

THE HUSBAND. Elka, what's wrong with you?

THE WIFE. I don't know who you are, but you are not my husband and I am not your wife and my name's not Elka. I have no name.

THE HUSBAND. Your name is Elka!

THE WIFE. *(approaches a shoe, reaches in and tastes)* Butter. I thought so. They're all filled with butter.

THE HUSBAND. Elka, stop this nonsense. Let's leave.

THE WIFE. Get away from me. Get away. You will not take me from this place. I see.

THE HUSBAND. Elka –

THE WIFE. I finally see.

(to audience) And, I did.

THE HUSBAND. *(to audience)* And that's how my life changed forever.

THE WIFE. Oh, of course, I knew exactly who he was, I just didn't know who I was. It's so hard to explain. You must understand, it's not as if you expect to stumble across 140 shoes filled with butter on a Sunday afternoon hunting trip in a remote region of Sweden. I was thinking about what I would make for dinner. And then –

THE HUSBAND. She left me. Not precisely…but in that instant she went away.

*(**THE BEAR** creeps in and listens.)*

THE WIFE. – there they were. There it was. I'd never seen anything so odd so astonishing so incomprehensible in my life.

THE HUSBAND. She changed, right before my eyes.

THE WIFE. I understood everything in that moment, by understanding...nothing. God, that sounds pretentious.

THE AUDIENCE MEMBER. You have no idea.

THE HUSBAND. *(to WIFE)* I'm calling the authorities.

THE WIFE. *(to HUSBAND)* I'm born again.

THE HUSBAND. What?

THE WIFE. I'm a baby. A new-born.

THE HUSBAND. *(to audience)* Do you see what I mean? So, I called for help.

(He calls on a cell phone.)

*(**ALF KJAELLSTROEM** enters, on telephone.)*

ALF KJAELLSTROEM. Alf Kjaellstroem, Provincial Spokesmen and Director of Heavy Equipment, how can I help you? Yes. Yes. No. Outrageous. High heels?

THE HUSBAND. Yes, there are high heels.

ALF KJAELLSTROEM. Boots?

THE HUSBAND. Yes.

ALF KJAELLSTROEM. Are there...tap shoes?

THE HUSBAND. *(not to his wife, but incredulously)* Are there tap shoes?

THE WIFE. Of course, there are tap shoes.

THE BEAR. It's not easy for an expatriate American Brown Bear to find tap shoes in Central Sweden.

*(**THE WIFE** taps a rimshot using a pair of tap shoes.)*

ALF KJAELLSTROEM. I'll...notify the media.

THE WRITER. I was writing a play when I got the call.

ALF KJAELLSTROEM. "If we knew who had done this we could make them clean this mess up...

THE WRITER. ...Alf Kjaellstroem, a province spokesman told The Associated Press today."

ALF KJAELLSTROEM. "It's not going to be pretty when the butter starts to rot. And, we have to wait for the snow so we can get up there with the snowmobile."

(a long pause)

How was that? Was that a good quote? Will I get in the papers?

THE WRITER. Is that all you can think about? Rotten butter and snowmobiles?

ALF KJAELLSTROEM. Slacker! Some of us have responsibility. Some of us take that responsibility seriously. Rotting butter is a serious problem. Children are starving, for example.

THE WRITER. That's what this is about. It's a statement about competing human appetites.

THE WIFE. I don't think this is about appetite.

THE BEAR. No, it's not.

ALF KJAELLSTROEM. Someone has to clean this mess up.

THE WRITER. It's not a mess, it's art. The triumph of consumerism and the death of agrarian society.

THE WIFE. The absurdity of modernity.

THE HUSBAND. The end of my life.

THE BEAR. It's private!

ALF KJAELLSTROEM. This is not art. This is not art. This is nuisance. The butter will attract pests and bears.

THE BEAR. That is so ursist.

THE WRITER. It should be left undisturbed.

ALF KJAELLSTROEM. *(Hitlerian)* It's the butter. The butter will rot. The butter will attract the worst elements. We must do something about the butter.

THE HUSBAND. He's right. The butter will rot.

THE WIFE. He's a fascist. The butter is supposed to rot.

THE BEAR. The butter was the most difficult part of the piece.

THE WIFE. The butter is the essence of the piece.

THE BEAR. It's such a delicate medium, and –

THE WIFE. It's such a difficult medium, and –

(*almost simultaneously*)

She just has –

THE WIFE. I just have –

THE WIFE & THE BEAR. Such big paws.

(*Pause. They share a meaningful moment.*)

THE HUSBAND. We must leave now.

THE WIFE. No!

THE HUSBAND. This will end badly. I feel it.

(*He exits.*)

ALF KJAELLSTROEM. Your job is to report the news, not argue with me about artistic expression.

THE WRITER. You are dangerous.

ALF KJAELLSTROEM. You need me. Come, we'll be famous.

(*He exits. Pause.*)

THE WRITER. When I reported it, I realized it was similar to a piece done by a Chinese Artist in 1996. His name was Yu Xiuzhen and his exhibit "Shoes With Butter," was installed in the Tibetan mountains in China.

(**THE BEAR** *looks directly at him, and speaks.*)

THE BEAR. Excuse me.

THE WRITER. (*screams*) Who are you?

THE BEAR. I'm...a bear. Her name is *Yin* Xiuzhen, not *Yu* Xiuzhen. And, *she* is a *woman*, not a man.

THE WRITER. What? You – you're the artist?

THE BEAR. Yes, I'm the artist. No, that's not correct. Yin Xuizhen is the artist. I am her admirer.

THE WRITER. But, you're a bear.

THE BEAR. Yes, I know.

THE WRITER. I already put it on the wires.

THE WIFE. It must be corrected.

THE WRITER. You're telling me my most widely published work has an attribution error –

THE WIFE & THE BEAR. – and is sexist.

THE WRITER. Dammit! Can we let it slide?

THE BEAR. Growl.

THE WRITER. Correction, Buttered Shoes Story: "In an October 9th story about the discovery of 70 pairs of shoes filled with butter on a Swedish mountain, The Associated Press erroneously reported the name and sex of a Chinese Artist who did a similar installation in China. The female artist is…

THE BEAR & THE WIFE. Yin Xiuzhen,

THE WRITER. not Yu Xiuzhen."

THE BEAR. Millions read the story,

THE WIFE. but no one read the correction.

THE WRITER. I'm a failure.

THE BEAR. It was private.

THE WIFE. I know.

THE HUSBAND. *(enters with* **ALF***)* Help me. Help me get her away from here.

ALF KJAELLSTROEM. I'm sorry, Madam. This is a crime scene. You must leave.

THE WIFE. I'm not leaving. I'm never leaving.

THE HUSBAND. Elka, enough is enough.

THE WIFE. I told you, my name's not Elka. *You* must leave. This place is private. It's for her.

THE HUSBAND & ALF KJAELLSTROEM. For who?

THE WRITER. For *whom.*

THE HUSBAND & ALF KJAELLSTROEM. For whom?

THE WIFE. For Yin. For the Artist, Yin Xiuzhen. Don't you see?

(pointing to **THE BEAR***)*

She loves her. This is a love poem to Yin.

THE BEAR. Yes.

THE WIFE. We were never supposed to see it. All of you must leave.

THE BEAR. You understand.

THE WIFE. But…can I stay?

(a realization)

Can I stay and be her?

THE BEAR. Would you?

THE WIFE. My name is Yin!

THE BEAR. Yin. *Yin.*

(moving towards **THE WIFE***)*

Oh, Yin.

THE HUSBAND. It's attacking my wife.

(He raises gun.)

THE WIFE. No, darling, don't.

(She lunges in front of **THE BEAR**. **HUSBAND** *shoots* **WIFE***.)*

THE HUSBAND. ELKA!

(He drops gun and runs to her, cradling her in his arms.)

THE BEAR. Yin. Yin! ROAR!

ALF KJAELLSTROEM. *(picking up gun)* I told you the butter would attract bears.

THE WRITER. No!

*(***ALF*** shoots* **THE BEAR**. **THE WRITER** *grabs the rifle from* **ALF**. *Then, an anguished cry.)*

You madman!

(Pause. Then, to audience.)

I was so enraged that I wrote a political drama called *The Husband, The Wife, The Fascist and The Bear.*

THE AUDIENCE MEMBER. Oh, God!

THE WRITER. Audiences had difficulty accepting the premise. So, I started over, from scratch. This time, opera was my inspiration, but I hate opera and I'm not a musician. It was turgid.

THE BEAR. Declaratory.

ALF KJAELLSTROEM. Incomprehensible.

THE HUSBAND. Well, we thought it was interesting,

THE WIFE. But, pretentious.

THE AUDIENCE MEMBER. It's awful.

(She leaves her seat.)

It's awful!

THE WRITER. Shut up!

(He shoots **THE AUDIENCE MEMBER** *and she falls in the aisle. Horrified, he drops the gun, which fires again.)*

Dammit!

*(***THE ARTISTIC DIRECTOR** *emerges from the audience, cradling* **THE AUDIENCE MEMBER** *in his arms.)*

THE ARTISTIC DIRECTOR. You shot her.

THE WRITER. Sorry.

THE ARTISTIC DIRECTOR. She's a subscriber.

THE WRITER. I'm sorry. I – I have trouble with exposition. I'm sorry.

(He cries. They look at him.)

Where were we?

THE BEAR. I just got shot.

THE WRITER. You madman!

(He rushes to **THE BEAR,** *and cradles her in his arms.* **ALF KJAELLSTROEM** *moves upstage, perhaps to a raised platform. The end of Puccini's* Nessun Dorma, *from* Turandot, *begins to play. It is lip-synched or sung by the characters. The style is operatic and melodramatic.)*

THE BEAR, THE WIFE & THE AUDIENCE MEMBER.

Il nome suo nessun saprà, e noi doverm, ahimè, morir, morir.

(They struggle for life.)

THE WRITER, THE HUSBAND & THE ARTISTIC DIRECTOR.
Dilegua, o notte! Tramontate, stella. Tramontate, stella!

THE WRITER, THE HUSBAND, THE ARTISTIC DIRECTOR & ALF KJAELLSTROEM.
All'alba vincerò! Vincerò! Vincerò!

*(***THE BEAR, THE WIFE*** and* **THE AUDIENCE MEMBER** *die.)*

(As orchestration rises after the Aria, **ALF KJAELL-STROEM** *emerges, as if giving a speech to a large crowd.)*

ALF KJAELLSTROEM. It's the butter. The butter. The butter will rot. The butter will rot. The butter will rot. The butter will rot. The butter will rot! THE BUTTER WILL ROOOOOOOOT!

(Speech and orchestration end simultaneously. Blackout.)

End of Play

OFF-OFF-BROADWAY FESTIVAL PLAYS

TWENTY-FOURTH SERIES
The Last Cigarette   Flight of Fancy   Physical Therapy   Nothing in the World Like It
The Price You Pay   Pearls Ophelia   A Significant Betrayal

TWENTY-FIFTH SERIES
Strawberry Fields   Sin Inch Adjustable   Evening Education   Hot Rot
A Pink Cadillac Nightmare   East of the Sun and West of the Moon

TWENTY-SIXTH SERIES
Tickets, Please!   Someplace Warm   The Test   A Closer Look
A Peace Replaced   Three Tables

TWENTY-SEVENTH SERIES
Born to Be Blue   The Parrot   Flights   A Doctor's Visit
Three Questions   The Devil's Parole

TWENTY-EIGHTH SERIES
Along for the Ride   A Low-Lying Fog   Blueberry Waltz   The Ferry
Leaving Tangier   Quick & Dirty (A Subway Fantasy)

TWENTY-NINTH SERIES
All in Little Pieces   The Casseroles of Far Rockaway   Feet of Clay
The King and the Condemned   My Wife's Coat   The Theodore Roosevelt Rotunda

THIRTIETH SERIES
Defacing Michael Jackson   The Ex   Kerry and Angie   Outside the Box
Picture Perfect   The Sweet Room

THIRTY-FIRST SERIES
Le Supermarché   Libretto   Play #3   Sick   Pischer   Relationtrip

THIRTY-SECOND SERIES
Opening   Circuit Breakers   Bright. Apple. Crush.
The Roosevelt Cousins, Thoroughly Sauced   Every Man   The Good Book

THIRTY-THIRD SERIES
F*cking Art   Ayravana Flies *or* A Pretty Dish   The Thread Men
The Dying Breed   The Grave   Juniper; Jubilee

THIRTY-FOURTH SERIES
Drop   The Education of Macoloco   realer than that
The Student   Thucydides   Just Knots

THIRTY-FIFTH SERIES
White Embers   Skin Deep   Pigskin
Dance Lessons   The Mud is Thicker in Mississippi   The Bear (a tragedy)

SAMUELFRENCH.COM

OTHER TITLES AVAILABLE FROM SAMUEL FRENCH

BE A GOOD LITTLE WIDOW

Bekah Brunstetter

Dramatic Comedy /2m, 2f / Interior

Young wife Melody has never been to a funeral – until her husband dies in a plane crash. Expected to instantly assume proper widowhood, Melody is left to wonder, what's the right way to grieve? Fortunately, her mother-in-law is a professional. Widow, that is. Under her guidance, Melody must try her best to be a good little widow. A sad comedy about loss and longing.

"Delicately satisfying…[Ms. Brunstetter] writes fresh, unfussy dialogue and characters who earn their laughs and emotional moments by honest means."
–*The New York Times*

"Bekah Brunstetter's powerful new play marries the humor and sadness of grief. Brunstetter's words pierce the soul, and she makes the depths of the human experience profoundly relatable…Her multidimensional characters' pain radiated through my veins, and at the end, I just wanted to feel it all over again. Critic's Pick."
– *Backstage*

OTHER TITLES AVAILABLE FROM SAMUEL FRENCH

EXTINCTION

Gabe McKinley

Dramatic Comedy / 2m, 2f

Two college buddies whose annual outing of male-bonding and debauchery veers precipitously off course when unmet expectations spiral into a volatile showdown. A darkly funny drama exploring the evolution of friendships - and the lengths to which we go to save them from falling into extinction.

"*Extinction* is intimate theatre at its edgy best!"
— *Examiner.com*

"Gabe McKinley's *Extinction* is the creative meat of a truly talented writer."
— *Variety*

"*Extinction* is USA Choice Grade A theatre"
— *Stage Scene LA*

"Uniquely unsettling"
— *LA Times*

"New playwright Gabe McKinley's dialogue is a real crowd-pleaser. Fast-paced, contemporary, and deliciously cruel."
— *BroadwayWorld.com*

OTHER TITLES AVAILABLE FROM SAMUEL FRENCH

CHRISTMAS SHORTS

Matt Hoverman

Collection of short plays / Holiday Comedy

A celebrated Winner of the 2009 Samuel French Off Off Broadway Short Play Festival, playwright Matt Hoverman brings an evening of hilarious short holiday comedies to the stage. A wonderful alternative for theatres tired of mounting the traditional seasonal play, *Christmas Shorts* offers five original plays that humorously comment on holiday themes: family, the nativity, Xmas cards, and elves. An outstanding Christmas collection for any theatre!

Included are the plays: *Going Home, The Christmas Witch, Xmas Cards, Nativity,* and the Samuel French Festival award-winning play *The Student.*

OTHER TITLES AVAILABLE FROM SAMUEL FRENCH

ACCIDENTS HAPPEN

J. Michael DeAngelis
Pete Barry
& John Dowgin

Collection of short plays / Comedy

Winner! 2009 NJACT Perry Award for Outstanding Production of an Original Play

Seven of The Porch Room's best short plays collected together into an evening of comedy that proves that no matter what you plan for - accidents happen. Shorts include:

ACCIDENTS HAPPEN - Please beware of all safety procedures and take note of the emergency exits.

NINE POINT EIGHT METERS PER SECOND PER SECOND - Balthazar Kent, ejected from an airplane, tries to regain control of his life through his cellphone.

REUNION SPECIAL - A desperate former child actor reunites with his now adult co-stars at a funeral.

THE CLIVE WAY - A motivational speaker mistakenly tries to empower a group of newly rehabilitated anger-management patients.

HANGMAN - A budding teenage philosopher-scientist searches for the truth by experimenting on his friend with a hallucinogenic cocktail.

TRICKS OF THE TRADE - Ralph teaches Eddie how to sell your soul for success.

THE BANDERSCOTT - An infomercial marketer is pitched an astonishing product.

The shorts can be performed together as a full-length show or on their own as one acts.

OTHER TITLES AVAILABLE FROM SAMUEL FRENCH

SMALL TALK

Eric Fallen

This collection of eight 10 minute plays include:

PERFECT WEATHER (2m) – When a strange man interrupts Jim's meditative morning ritual, what begins with small talk about the weather, soon devolves into a bizarre interrogation.

THE MERRY-GO-ROUND (1 m, 1f) – After a vigorous morning of work, two porn actors get lost in a circular conversation.

COMMUNION (1m, 2f) – When a dying man's request for a strawberry milkshake is denied by his long-suffering wife, the couple descend into a battle that could be their last.

THE MONSTER (2m) – A motorcycle salesman uses all the usual tricks to lure his customer in, but a strange and violent story prevents him from closing the deal.

BASIC PLUMBING (2m) – A small town library is the setting for a stand-off between an up-tight librarian and the local madman.

THE DRIVING RANGE (1 m, 1f) – While an instructor leads a woman through the basics of the golf swing, an underlying tension threatens to throw them both off their game.

BEHIND THE WHEEL (2m) – A man begs his brother to save him from despair by letting his father-in-law die.

THE INCLUSION (1m , 1f) – When a woman invites an old friend to her jewelry store to help him find the best diamond for his fiancé, it eventually becomes clear that he wants more than her advice.